Love's Trail in Kenya

D to the Fourth Books & Scripts, LLC

ISBN: 979-8-9907023-5-6 (paperback)

D to the Fourth Books & Scripts, LLC

Stanley, NC

United States of America

TABLE OF CONTENTS

.

Love's Trail in Kenya

Dewey Dellinger

Chapter 1

Like an angry dragon slithering from its cave, spewing flame and brimstone, fire spat from the mouth of the machine gun as the ammunition that fed its belly snaked up and into the chamber. The rat a tat tat of the angry serpent was silencing its foes, but it could not silence the voice inside his head. The only thing Gordon could hear was, "Why wasn't it me?" Gordon was the older brother; he should have been the one to die.

Gordon's thoughts and emotions changed as rapidly as the ammunition that entered the gun: he and his younger brother Grant helping their father on the cattle ranch in Wyoming, moving to Colorado to start a new cattle ranch near Pueblo, repairing the sod house after storm damage, hunting in the Colorado mountains, eating watermelons on watermelon day in Rocky Ford where he and his brother spat watermelon seeds at each other. The tragedies also flooded his mind: their parents taken to a sanitarium for tuberculosis where they later died, he and his brother trying to make it on their own in Bailey, Colorado, moving to Tennessee to live with their maternal aunt whom they had not met previously, himself being drafted into this horrible war, his underaged brother volunteering, and his brother getting killed.

Gordon couldn't stop his younger brother, Grant, from volunteering for the war no matter how hard he tried. Why did younger siblings always have to try to outdo their older siblings? It was probably human nature. The older sibling would forge the path; the younger would travel it further. Both brothers were in the 30th Infantry Division, which was attached to the British Expeditionary Forces. Both fought in the Battle of Cambrai. Both fought in the Battle of the Selle; only one survived. The only object left in the world that he had of his brother's was his dog tag.

Gordon learned of his brother's death barely an hour ago. A skin and bones private had made his way through the hellish trench maze to inform him. Gordon didn't know if the private was a friend of Grant's, whether he drew the short stick, or whether the private was hoping his hell on earth would be ended by a German sniper. The Great War had a way of snuffing the interest out of life. Gordon knew of soldiers who would search among the fallen bodies for a cigarette without giving much thought to dying; they were more interested in a smoke to break the boredom or to soothe their nerves.

No sooner had the private delivered the news than their sergeant informed them they were in danger of being cut off from the rest of the troops. They would have to retreat now, but German soldiers were already beginning to overtake their flanks. The sergeant didn't know if any of them would make it out alive, but he needed two volunteers: volunteers for a suicide mission. Gordon couldn't even remember raising his hand to volunteer. The only way he found out that he had raised his hand was when the second volunteer grasped his shoulder and gave him a *let's give 'em hell til they kill us* look. Each would man a machine gun. Ordinarily two men manned a single machine gun. One would feed the ammunition belt while the other fired. Today, though, each would man his own machine gun. The sergeant was looking for a sacrificial distraction that would buy them perhaps one minute of retreat.

The clanging noise of a bullet grazing his helmet interrupted his thoughts. German soldiers were gaining ground. Gordon swept the machine gun in an arc halting their advance and killing one before he could throw a hand grenade. The dragon kept belching fire and smoke, quelling its foes one by one. But even a dragon has but so much fire. As the last bullet burst out of the machine gun, Gordon unholstered his M1911 Colt pistol and picked off seven German soldiers who were brave enough to venture toward him. Gordon was an expert sharpshooter, and he had been awarded the rifle expert badge as well as the pistol expert badge. His sharpshooting skills would come in handy today. Tossing the empty pistol aside, Gordon grabbed his Enfield rifle. More troops advanced cautiously, hugging the ground, but he was able to pick off one with each cartridge. Gordon picked up another Enfield from a nearby fallen soldier just as several enemy soldiers charged his position. He emptied the rifle, but one German soldier had made his way to Gordon. Dodging the lunge of his foe's bayonet, he slammed the butt of the rifle into the German's unprotected head. More enemy soldiers began to advance toward him. When Gordon finally looked over to the other machine gun, he saw the second volunteer dead. He picked up the body and hurled it away from the machine gun, uncovering another dead machine gunner underneath. Gordon rolled the body away and began firing the second machine gun. When the gun finally emptied, no soldiers advanced toward him. He doubted that he had killed all of them. More than likely, they went around him. His father told him one time, "Sometimes you just have to plow around the stump." Gordon was the stump they went around, which meant he was deep in enemy territory.

"I can't stay here," he mumbled to himself. Picking up his Enfield, some extra ammunition, and a pack of cigarettes from a fallen comrade, he slinked from cover to cover until he entered a heavily wooded area. For over an hour, he ran from tree to tree, hearing gunshots and explosions no matter how far he ran. Mud and dirt covered his uniform and face. His chest heaved for air, and fatigue enveloped him, sending chills of fear throughout his body. The struggle for air reminded him of the tear gas mask he had worn at one point during the Battle of Cambrai as gas hung in the air around him. The panic that settled within him seemed palpable, causing him to run without thinking. As he rounded the bottom of a hill, he came across an African soldier carrying a Lewis gun. Although the lightweight machine gun was portable, the man had to have considerable strength to swing the barrel toward him with such ease. He had barely swung around his rifle in time.

The two men's weapons were trained on each other, the Enfield rifle on the African and the Lewis gun on him. Suddenly the thought of Grant entered his mind, and Gordon was finished. Releasing his hold on the Enfield, the rifle fell to the ground. "Go ahead. Shoot." The African soldier blinked, and Gordon noticed for the first time that the African was standing over the body of a fallen African soldier.

"Are you German?" asked the African. "You don't have the

same accent as other British soldiers."

"I'm American, but it doesn't matter. Just shoot me."

"Why do you want to die?"

"Is that your friend?" Gordon nodded his head as if pointing to the fallen soldier.

"Yes. His name is … was Chima."

"I found out today that my younger brother was killed. He was underaged and shouldn't have been here. I was the one who was drafted. I was the one who was supposed to protect my brother, but I failed him. I failed my parents. I should have had his death; he should have had my life. Kill me, damn it!"

The African soldier lowered the Lewis gun. "Maybe all you say is true, but you can't trade places with your brother now, no matter how much you want. I'm not going to kill an ally. I may need that ammunition before today is finished. Besides, I figure that before today is over, the Germans will honor your request. How did you get separated from your unit?"

Gordon quickly explained the chain of events that had brought him into the woods.

"My name is Kagiso. What is yours?"

"Gordon. Gordon Powell."

"Well, Gordon Powell, shall we find the Germans before they find us?"

"Let me help you bury your friend first."

"The Bible says to let the dead bury the dead. If we stay here much longer, we too will be dead, and I don't know how we will be able to bury him then. Let's go. Vengeance is a better substitute than burial."

Gordon and Kagiso set out toward where they thought the allied lines would be, even though the smoky haze that hung over the hell they were in obscured their sense of direction. They walked in silence, each dwelling on their own thoughts. Another hour had passed when they heard shouts in German.

"Do you know what they're saying?" asked Kagiso.

"No, but they sound pretty riled up."

Gordon and Kagiso furtively approached the sounds of spoken German, seeking cover behind a large boulder. They poked their heads from each side of the boulder. Gordon saw about ten German soldiers gathered around an injured British officer, but several more German soldiers were in a large foxhole, and a machine gun stood just outside of the foxhole.

"If you wish to die, this is as good a time as any," whispered Kagiso.

One of the German soldiers raised his bayonet to skewer the British officer. The officer held up his arm and pleaded for his life. As the German began the downward descent with his bayonet, Gordon quickly took aim from beside of the boulder and killed the bayonet-bearer before he could kill the officer. Gordon shot another soldier before what had happened sunk in. After the second German soldier was shot, the Germans were fully aware they were being attacked. One of the German soldiers was foolish enough to try to kill the British officer rather than take cover, and Gordon quickly shot him. The remaining seven or so Germans ran behind cover. Six Germans scrambled out of the foxhole and ran towards cover on the opposite side of the seven. Kagiso was able to mow down two of them with the Lewis gun before they were able to reach the safety of cover. One German ran from the foxhole to the machine gun and tried to lug it back to the foxhole, but Kagiso was able to stop him before he had a chance to reach the machine gun. There still remained about thirteen German soldiers firing from two different directions. Kagiso sprayed both sides with machine gun fire. The British officer crawled on his belly along the ground trying to find some safety. When the drum magazine in the Lewis gun finally emptied, one of the German soldiers in the group of six prepared to lob a hand grenade. The soldier was exposed just long enough for Gordon to use his sharpshooting skills to shoot the soldier. The resulting blast killed the group of six.

About seven German soldiers remained. Kagiso had replaced the circular drum magazine of the Lewis gun with a new one holding ninety-seven rounds. Kagiso gave a nod to Gordon, who read the intention behind the nod. Both stepped out from behind the cover of the boulder and, with Kagiso spraying bullets, advanced toward cover closer to the group of Germans. One German soldier stood up and tried to quickly lock aim on Kagiso, but Gordon shot him. Two more Germans ran from their cover to the foxhole, but Kagiso trained the Lewis gun on them and killed them before they could reach the foxhole. Gordon fired his rifle to keep the Germans' heads down. Both Gordon and Kagiso ran out of ammunition at about the same time. Gordon quickly attached his bayonet to his rifle, and Kagiso picked up a rifle with a bayonet already attached from a fallen German soldier. Three Germans charged from behind their cover brandishing bayonets. Gordon stabbed one of the soldiers but was tackled by the other soldier. Gordon and the German soldier wrestled and vied for position. Meanwhile, Kagiso slammed the butt of the rifle into the head of the soldier he fought. Both Gordon and the German soldier wrestled on the ground. The German had a twenty- or thirty-pound weight advantage over Gordon. Soon, the German was able to get on top of Gordon, and he pulled out his knife and swung it toward Gordon's chest. Although Gordon managed to grab the German's arm on the downward swing, the knife, aided by the German's weight, was making its way closer and closer to Gordon's heart. The knife was an inch away from plunging into Gordon's heart. Sweat from the German's face dropped into Gordon's face and eyes, clouding his vision. The pungent odor of the German's breath forced its way into Gordon's nostrils. Gordon's arms were about to give way under the constant pressure exerted by the German. The German lowered his head and flashed an *I won, you son of a bitch* smile so that Gordon could clearly see the victor before he died. With the German's mouth mere inches from Gordon's eyes, Gordon rammed his head into the teeth and nose of the German. The headbutt stunned him long enough for Gordon to grab his own knife at his leg with his free hand while the other hand continued holding back the German's knife. Before the German's presence could return, Gordon had his knife and swung it, plunging it to the hilt in the German's neck. As Gordon rolled the dead body off of him, he caught sight of the fourth German standing over him thrusting his bayonet downward. From seemingly out of nowhere, Kagiso's bayonet gored the German. Although the bayonet's trajectory was deflected, the deflection wasn't enough for the bayonet to miss Gordon. They bayonet punched into his side and embedded itself in the ground, pinning Gordon.

A yelp of pain reverberated through the air. Gordon was surprised at the dimensionality of the sound. Once he saw Kagiso though, he understood the added dimension of the sound. The soldier that Kagiso had battered with the butt of his rifle had not been killed. The German was on his knees with blood pouring from his head. He had managed to swing his rifle into Kagiso's leg, and Kagiso was on the ground, writhing in pain. The German fought his way to a standing, though wobbly, position. With the bayonet tip aimed at Kagiso, the soldier prepared to fall, driving the bayonet into Kagiso. Gordon pulled out his Colt pistol, aimed it at the German's head, prayed there was at least one bullet left in the chamber, and pulled the trigger. A shot rang out from the pistol, and the bullet struck the German between the eyes. The force was enough to knock him backwards, and he dropped the bayonet harmlessly to the ground as he collapsed.

With the fighting stopped, the British officer clawed his way, one handful of dirt at a time, toward Gordon and Kagiso. When he reached Gordon, he tried to pull the bayonet, still attached to the rifle, from Gordon's side. His strength sapped; he couldn't budge the bayonet. With Gordon's own help, the two struggled for a couple of minutes before finally unpinning Gordon from the ground. Gordon painfully rolled onto his knees. He stood up and the blood drained from his face leaving in its place a pale blue tint. Gordon could feel his consciousness fading as if being pulled by gravity. Gravity pulled at his body as well, and he collapsed, unconscious, to the ground.

Gordan wasn't sure how long he was unconscious. He still couldn't force his eyes open to see what was happening, but he felt a cool pressure on his face that beckoned him back to reality. When he finally opened his eyes, he could see the British officer applying cool water from a canteen with a cloth to his face. Gordon looked over to find Kagiso, still on the ground but at least not writhing in pain.

After fifteen minutes, Gordon tried, successfully, to stand again. He helped Kagiso to a standing position and found a rifle that he could use as a crutch. Lastly, he turned his attention to the British lieutenant, who was at least sitting and leaning his back against a rock while smoking a cigarette.

"I hope you don't mind," apologized the lieutenant. I took one while you were unconscious."

"Not at all. Where are you injured?"

"I have a gunshot wound on the opposite side of my body of your stab wound. I was beaten badly during questioning, and I think I have a few broken ribs. I think I can stand though."

"I'll try to help you stand. We need to get out of here and try to make it to the allied lines. With a little effort, the lieutenant was able to stand. Now that all three were upright, they limped and trudged in the direction they had been traveling before the encounter with the Germans. They traveled into the night; the haze had lifted enough that the moon provided some illumination. They kept silent in case any Germans were nearby.

Around midnight, they heard, "Who goes there? Hold your hands high and keep them where I can see them."

The three did as they were ordered, and two sentries appeared out of the darkness. "Sprechen Sie Deutsch?" questioned one of the sentries.

"About as much as you do?" answered Gordon in a Tennessee accent he picked up from where his aunt lived.

"Oh, a yank, eh? If you're part of the thirtieth infantry, what are you doing this far away?"

"Corporal," answered the lieutenant in an upper-class British accent, "we are in desperate need of proper medical attention. If you would be so kind as to show us to a casualty clearing station."

"Yes sir. I'm sorry, lieutenant. I didn't notice you." The corporal called over a few privates who led the three to the field hospital. From there, the three were transferred to a base hospital in the rear, far from the front lines.

While recuperating, the three got to know each other well. Kagiso would often tell stories of his home in Kenya and of the African savanna. The stories kept Gordon going. They kept him, as best they could, from thinking of his brother. The savanna, as described by Kagiso, showed the unforgiving aspect of nature. It matched Gordon's feeling of being unforgiven.

By the time the three were discharged less than a month later, the Great War had ended. Although American troops would remain in Europe for six months or more, Gordon was sent stateside due to his injury. He came to Europe with his brother. He returned alone. One month made the difference between Grant being alive versus getting killed. It was like the savanna that Kagiso described. To Gordon, the world seemingly consisted of either predators or prey, and one decision could make the difference between life and death.

Chapter 2

Sarah Jacobs, cultural anthropologist for the Museum of Colorado History, sat in the museum's meeting room with several other staff members as they waited for the museum's director, Sean Marshall, to arrive and start the meeting. The chairs in the room were large, and at five foot four, Sarah's feet could not touch the floor unless she sat on the end of the chair. Most people described her as cute, probably because she was slim without much of an hour-glass frame, which was fine with her. Her shoulder-length, layered, auburn-colored hair complimented her light skin tone. She was at the age most women held at, twenty-nine.

Just as Sarah turned to chat with Inez Martinez, the museum archivist, Sean arrived. As usual, he was precisely five minutes late. Sarah swore he did this on purpose. Sean was in his early forties. He almost always wore a white shirt, gray pants, and red tie. To Sarah, he seemed like he should have been a Vice President in a Fortune 500 company instead of a museum director.

"Good morning, everyone," greeted Sean. "As you are aware, our Board of Directors recently decided to revise the focus for our collections." Although that was not news to anyone, the room still filled with the chatter of opinions, mostly against the new focus. "Now folks, I know change can be difficult, but the Board establishes our focus. Let's view this as an opportunity to increase our visibility and to educate more of the citizenry about Colorado history and culture. I have a list here of exhibits to be culled in order to make room for other exhibits that better reflect the museum's new focus. Sarah, I would like for you to double check the list to make sure that nothing is listed here by mistake."

"Of course, Sean."

"Once everything is verified, turn the list over to our archivist, Inez, who will dispose of or redistribute the materials as appropriate."

As Sean began to address the new marketing campaign, Sarah began to think about her time working at the museum. Sarah began working at the museum shortly after graduating with her master's degree in cultural anthropology. The job was stable; her co-workers were friendly, but she couldn't say that she really enjoyed what she was doing. Realistically, with a master's degree in cultural anthropology, she couldn't find a better job. But she felt that almost anyone could handle the job she did. She wanted to do field work in cultural anthropology, but those kinds of jobs were practically nonexistent. Sarah's attention returned to the meeting at hand, and Sean was now discussing the need to attract new donors. Fortunately, the meeting lasted less than an hour. That was one of Sean's redeeming qualities; he didn't drag out meetings.

The list of exhibits to cull comprised almost half of the current exhibits. The Board of Directors were definitely serious about changing the focus. Sarah began the monotonous task of double-checking the list. She was fairly certain that this was merely an exercise that Sean could use to say that the museum had done its due diligence in culling the pieces that did not meet the new focus. Even if she found something that she believed should remain, she would probably be overruled. When Sarah arrived at the twelfth item on the list, she paused. Sarah had seen this exhibit before, if one could call it an exhibit, but she had not paid particular attention to it. The exhibit consisted of a picture with a very brief description. The picture was of a World War I veteran and African hunter. It was an old black and white picture of a man who could have passed for a cowboy from the old west. He looked to have dark brown hair from what she could tell of the old picture, a bushy mustache, and an old hat. The hat wasn't quite like any of the other cowboy hats she had seen. It was wider brimmed, sort of like the hat of an old Canadian Mountie or a drill sergeant, but not exactly those either. Sarah understood why this piece was on the list to be culled. Rather than being a part of a larger exhibit, such as war veterans, for instance, the picture was an isolated piece.

As Sarah studied the picture and its description, Sean walked by, hesitated, and approached her. "How's the list coming, Sarah?"

Sarah was so engrossed in the picture that Sean's voice startled her. "Oh. Fine, but I notice that you want to cull this piece."

"Yes." Although Sean's face was for the most part expressionless, Sarah thought there was a *what's your point* look behind it somewhere.

"The information on this piece says that this man, Gordon

Powell, was a veteran of World War I and lived in Wyoming and Colorado."

"So," replied Sean.

"It just seems as though it would be nice to have something on a veteran who lived in this state, even if it were part of a larger collection on veterans."

"It doesn't fit our focus anymore, Sarah. Besides, Gordon Powell was a hunter in Africa in the 1920s. When the museum first got this piece, it was very Hemingway-esque at the time, but it's dated now. This exhibit is also associated too much with colonialism and the killing of endangered species. It's just not popular with modern museum audiences." Sean walked off, apparently satisfied with his explanation.

Something about the picture spoke to Sarah, touched her. She wasn't quite sure what it was. Perhaps the sad eyes. Or, as Sean suggested, perhaps it was the Hemingway-esque appeal of the Lost Generation. The term was coined by the American writer Gertrude Stein to describe the directionless spirit of the group that entered adulthood during World War I and the Spanish Flu epidemic and had survived. The Lost Generation was a social generation, much like the Baby Boomers, Gen X, or millennials. This generation was perhaps the driving force for the Roaring Twenties. How she would have loved to study the cultural influences and impacts of this group first-hand. Sarah loved cultural anthropological research, which was not what she was doing in her museum job. Rather than telling people about the things she had just been thinking, she was looking at a list of objects to cull. Well, if she couldn't tell other people, she could at least satisfy her own curiosity.

Sarah made her way to the museum storeroom where Inez typically worked. "Hi, Inez."

Inez looked up and greeted Sarah with smiling eyes. Inez was in her early thirties and a few years older than Sarah. Inez was Sarah's best friend at the museum, and they talked often. They mostly kept their friendship at the museum, only occasionally going out for an after-work drink or an evening dinner. "Hi, Sarah. Did you come to talk, or is this business?"

"Business today, I'm afraid."

"Alright, how can I help you?"

"May I see if there are any other catalogued materials for this exhibit?"

"Sure. Let's see what you have."

Sarah handed Inez a piece of paper with the catalog reference number for the materials on Gordon Powell. Generally, not all of the materials were put on display. The unused materials were archived in the museum storeroom.

"Ok. Wait here, and I'll be right back with the materials." Inez disappeared behind rows of maze-like shelving behind her desk, which resembled the circulation desk of a library. That's appropriate, thought Sarah. After all, Inez did have a degree in library science. Within a couple of minutes, Inez returned, carrying a box. Sarah was a little disappointed as she saw the size of the box. She had hoped there would be a lot of information available on Gordon Powell. Inez placed the box in front of Sarah and opened the lid. "What do you think of the decision to cull the materials?"

Sarah rummaged through the box as she spoke. "I understand that museum collections must be updated for relevancy and for today's generation, but understanding the past is also important."

"Spoken like a true anthropologist."

"What do you think about the decision?"

Inez shrugged. "It doesn't much matter to me. I archive whatever the museum decides to carry."

"Spoken like a true librarian."

"What's in there?"

Sarah continued to rummage through the box as if her stirring the pile would magically add more materials or uncover something she hadn't already seen. "There are some additional pictures of Gordon Powell, a letter, a newspaper article, and a few pages ripped out of a diary."

"Pick something and read it."

"Hmm. Ok, let's start with the letter." Sarah picked up the letter, discolored over time. A stale scent wafted from the letter to her nose causing her to wrinkle her nose and blink. She focused intently on the cursive writing and the faded ink until her eyes adjusted enough to allow her to read the communication from a bygone era.

Dear beloved Grant,

This makes the second time I've written to you after you were killed. I'm sorry I haven't communicated with you more often. I've just been too ashamed to face the thought of you. I've carried the burden with me for years that it should have been you who lived, not me. That shame drove me to hunting man-eating cats in hopes they would kill me. I'm writing to you now because I've fallen in love, fallen hard. Unfortunately, she's an English aristocrat who's engaged to someone else. You wouldn't know what to think of her. She's not what you think of when you picture the daughter of an earl. She is like a lion that cannot be tamed, from her golden curls and mischievous green eyes to her unapologetic audacity and bold free-spiritedness. She's a wild, independent beauty. This is probably the last letter you will receive from me, but you don't need to worry about me any longer. Even though I may never be with her, she's made a profound and everlasting change in me. I appreciate my life now and have made peace with the horrors I experienced in The Great War. Until we see each other on the other side, know that I have forgiven myself and that I love you.

Your brother throughout eternity.

Gordon.

"I've never seen a letter to a dead person before," exclaimed Inez. What else is in there?"

Sarah pulled the diary pages out of the box. I think these are pages ripped from a diary. The pages are just as old as the letter."

Sarah took a whiff. "And they smell just as stale. The handwriting looks different though; it looks like the handwriting of a woman."

"Maybe it's from the woman mentioned in the letter."

"Perhaps." Sarah began to read.

Chapter 3

The woman woke up, desperately needing to urinate. The darkness in her tent told her that it was still night, but how late at night or how early in the morning. She willed herself to go back to sleep, hoping that the dawn would break soon. The fullness of her bladder made sleeping impossible though. I shouldn't have had so much wine to drink, she scolded herself. After another five minutes of tossing and turning, she knew she couldn't hold her urine any longer. She blindly felt nearby until her hand touched the lantern. Now, she just had to find some matches. As her eyes grew a little more accustomed to the darkness, she felt around some more, careful not to knock over the lantern. She didn't want lamp oil and urine wetting her tent. She finally found the matches, struck one, and touched it to the wick. She adjusted the wick, and the warm glow illuminated the inside of her tent.

Holding the lantern in front of her, she went out into the African night, finding that the moon and stars made the outdoors less dark than the inside of her tent. She walked a little way from her tent to a bush. Lifting her gown, she squatted behind the tent. She peed like an elephant, not very ladylike, but the relief was immediate. She was almost finished when she heard it, a noise like the brushing of an animal against the savanna grass. She immediately stood up and ran for a tree that she saw nearby. Her heart was pounding. The hair on her head and arms stood erect. She was breathless when she closed in on the tree. Leaping, she grabbed the tree trunk, skinning her legs. Clawing her way up the trunk, she reached a low-lying branch, which she used to climb to the next branch. Looking out, she saw the dark shape of an animal. She didn't know if she were far enough up in the tree or if the animal she saw could climb. The animal came closer to the tree, and without even realizing, she heard a scream. It took her a moment to realize that the scream came from her. Finally, she found control of her voice and shouted, "Help! Can anyone hear me? Help! There's a hyena!"

Looking in the direction of the tents, she saw dim lantern light in several of the tents. Finding Gordon's tent, she saw movement near the tent flap. A shirtless man charged out and ran toward the tree. Suddenly, he stopped and raised a rifle, pointing it into the night sky. He fired, and the animal scampered away at the gunfire. He casually walked to the tree she had climbed, and she noticed that others were now outside of their tents, talking in words she couldn't hear at this distance. Gordon was now at the base of the tree, and soon, several others made their way to where he was standing. She climbed down to the first branch, and Gordon held out his hand and helped her down. With the adrenaline rush gone, she felt the stinging in her legs.

Once she was on solid ground, the gentlemanly nature of Gordon turned to anger. "What were you thinking coming out alone in the dark? You should never go out at night by yourself. You're lucky you weren't killed. A hyena is much faster than a human, and if that had been a real hyena, you wouldn't have made it to the tree in time. Fortunately, what you saw was an aardwolf. They look like hyenas but only eat insects. This is twice now that you not only endangered your own life but the lives of others." Gordon looked around at the others who were gathered nearby. "Okay everyone, back to your tents."

The group of onlookers, including her fiancé, walked back to their tents, trancelike. She began to walk back on wobbly legs that had not yet overcome her fright. Once safely inside her tent, she heard rumbling around the firepit and the sound of more wood stoking the fire. With her legs now sturdy and her confidence returned, she exited her tent and made her way to the fire where she saw Gordon sitting on a log. He pulled out his flask and took a hearty swig of whatever was inside. She found a spot on the log beside of him, and both were quiet for a moment. Gordon glanced at her, and she erupted. "I'm not going to be intimidated by anyone or anything. You're not one to criticize. You're still letting the war ruin your life. You sit around waiting to die, but you're already dead inside."

Gordon made not the slightest of reactions at her reproach but replied in a calm, almost disengaged manner, "You have no idea what the war was like."

"You're right. I don't, but I do know a man who is dead inside when I see one."

Gordon's voice turned from calmness to mournfulness. "You don't understand. My brother was underaged. I was supposed to protect him. It should have been me who was killed, not him."

The anger inside of her turned to compassion. Inside of the fearless guide was another person, one who was hiding a shattered soul. She put her hand on his leg to comfort him, and it jerked at the compassion she offered. "But it wasn't. Your brother sacrificed his life so that others could live, including you. So, live your life to the fullest to honor your brother's sacrifice. Don't just throw your life away. Otherwise, your brother died for nothing, and that's when you should truly grieve."

Gordon seemed to measure his words as he spoke. You say I should choose life. The only time I truly feel alive is when I'm facing danger, facing death."

"You feel alive during those moments because those are the only times you are connected with the world. It's not danger that makes you feel alive; it is being connected."

A sneer formed on Gordon's mouth. "What about you?" he chided. "Do you feel connected?"

She started at the comment, involuntarily removing her hand from his leg.

"You're living a life and planning a marriage that you know will never make you happy."

Her reply was as involuntary as her removing her hand from his leg. "Maybe we're both in the same boat and just don't know how to get out."

Gordon chuckled. The response seemed incongruent with his

previous attitude. "I have to give it to you. You certainly are a bold one. I've never had anyone talk to me the way you do."

Her heart lightened. Gordon seemed to return to the stoic guide she was used to seeing, and she returned to the spirited woman he was used to seeing. "And I've never met a man who didn't give in to my wishes. You don't."

She and Gordon stared into each other's eyes, as if looking into each other's soul. Both reached out at the same time and held the other's hand. Slowly, they leaned in and kissed, but both quickly broke off.

"We've got an early day tomorrow," acquiesced Gordon. "We'd both better turn in, or we won't be worth a shit."

She smiled and could almost see the sparkle in her own eyes. "You Americans have a way with words."

Gordon returned her smile, "And you British have a way with kissing."

Chapter 4

Back in the museum storeroom, Sarah laid the pages neatly in the box.

"Wow! That was intense," marveled Inez. "I wonder where the rest of the diary is, and who is the woman?"

"I don't know, but I sure am interested to find out."

Inez picked up the newspaper article from inside the box. She briefly examined it and handed it to Sarah. "This newspaper article is dated 1950. Maybe it will shed some more light on who this woman was."

Sarah handled the old newspaper clipping with care. She wished she had thought to wear gloves so that the oil from her hands wouldn't damage the fragile paper more than its current state. She began to read the brief article aloud.

World War I hero Gordon Powell, who was also a famous hunter of man-eating cats and a safari guide, was gored by a rhino when he

attempted to stop a hunter from shooting the
rhino. He died within an hour from injuries
inflicted by the rhino. When learning of
Gordon Powell's death, Ernest Hemingway said,
"Gertrude Stein called us the lost
generation, a wandering, directionless
generation disenfranchised from life by the
Great War. Gordon was one of the few men I
knew from that Great War who was able to find
his way back.

"The story just can't end like this. There has to be more
somewhere." Sarah put the newspaper article into the box, closed the
lid and handed it to Inez to reshelve.

That night, Sarah had dinner at a local restaurant with her
boyfriend of two years, Wesley Baldwin. Wesley was six feet tall with
jet black hair that naturally formed a bedhead hairstyle. He was slim
with a slim face. Wesley was a journalist for an online news
organization, and they met when Wesley was doing a story. He had
contacted the museum to get some information on an article he was
writing and had been put in contact with Sarah. Wesley was generally
of a serious nature and very hard-working. He knew what he wanted
and that was to get a job as a reporter in what he considered to be a
more reputable news establishment.

Between bites of grilled salmon, Sarah was filling Wesley in on
her day. "I just hate to see the museum cull this collection on Gordon
Powell."

She took another bite of salmon, and Wesley took this interlude as an invitation to interject.

"I know you're a cultural anthropologist, but why does this particular piece mean so much to you?"

Sarah pondered Wesley's question as she chewed her salmon. "I think two reasons," she answered after swallowing and taking a sip of water. "The work I do at the museum is fine, but it's not what really interests me. I don't really use my anthropology degree at the museum. What I really miss is doing ethnographies.   That's   the research and observations of individuals or cultures."

Wesley smiled slightly. "We've been together long enough for me to know what an ethnography is. But be practical; interests don't pay the bills. Jobs do."

Sarah's eyes squinted as the inside of her eyebrows lowered, displaying her mild annoyance at Wesley's matter-of-fact advice. "That's easy to say when you have a job that you love that pays the bills. I'm just tired of the museum work and don't feel that I'm contributing in a meaningful way. I feel like I should be doing something more. I always wanted to help people learn about different cultures, but I'm not doing that."

Wesley sipped from his glass of wine during the slight admonishment. "Well, can you find a job that allows you to do what you want?"

"Not without a Ph.D., and I only have a master's degree. Even then, about the only job I could get would be a teaching job, and don't say I should have thought about that before majoring in cultural anthropology."

"I wouldn't dare, but teaching would certainly be helping people learn about different cultures."

"Unless the students are graduate students, most underclass college students only take anthropology to fill a general education requirement. The majority of the students I was in class with at college could have cared less about anthropology. Teaching in a university is not the only way to help people learn about different cultures. I want to do, not teach. Think about it in terms of your job. Teaching journalism students is a lot different than being a reporter."

"That's not a valid comparison. Teaching journalism is about getting students to learn how to write and report news. A journalist provides news and important information to the public. A job as a university professor of anthropology can be about teaching people about different cultures, not necessarily how to do the research, but I get your point."

Wesley always loved a good debate, thought Sarah. She almost wished that he wouldn't debate with her tonight though, but she had to admit that he usually did help her think through things more clearly when he went back and forth with her.

"You said there were two reasons this exhibit means so much to you. What is the other reason?"

"It's a personal reason. The letter that Gordon wrote really spoke to me. You remember that my grandfather was in the Vietnam War, and he suffered from PTSD. Some days, I would be so close to him, and then other days, it was like a wall went up, and he seemed distant and depressed. I can't help but wonder what our relationship would have been like if he had received the help he needed. If this

Gordon Powell overcame that, I'm curious to know how."

"Well, according to the letter, the reason was love."

"But I really want to know the story. I mean, my grandfather had love."

Wesley looked at a corner of the ceiling in the restaurant, and his face grew pensive. "I did an article on PTSD once. There are various degrees of PTSD, and everyone is different. What works for someone might not work for another."

"I'm neither a psychologist nor an investigative journalist, but there is a story there that I want to know the answer to."

"Well, I think a cultural anthropologist is probably a little of both."

This was one of the things that annoyed Sarah about Wesley. He was usually attentive, but sometimes he seemed a little patronizing. He always seemed to have the answer that he was more than willing to supply her. She supposed it was a hazard of his job. He never seemed to get out of the mode of reporting.

Sarah raised her head slightly and rubbed her chin. "For some reason, the name *Powell* really sticks in my head, as if I'm familiar with it."

Powell is a common name.

There he goes again, she thought, always having an explanation and the last word.

Later that night, when Sarah was back at home in her den, she grabbed a few photo albums and began to leaf through them. The first couple of albums she quickly put down. They contained pictures of a different time period than what she was looking for. When she found the one with pictures of her grandfather, she leafed through the pages more slowly until she found what she was looking for. She couldn't help but smile at the happy expression on her grandfather's face. The landscape in the picture was a little peculiar. It looked to be of Africa. There was a sign in the picture, and Sarah focused on it to make out the words. The sign read, *Powell's African Camp and Safari*. That was why the name *Powell* seemed familiar to her at the restaurant. She had seen the picture before, but what she really remembered was her grandfather talking about a trip he had taken to Africa, maybe in the eighties. She wasn't sure what year or decade the trip was, but he had described it as one of more the most peaceful times he had had since the Vietnam War. She was certain that he had said the name *Powell*. This couldn't be a coincidence. There had to be some connection with this camp and Gordon Powell. She just knew it.

The next morning, she was jittery as she went to Sean's office. Excitement, like electricity, pulsed through her body, and nervousness settled in the pit of her stomach. Although she had not drunk any coffee that morning, she was as wired as though she had consumed two large cups of dark, robust coffee. Even the knocking noise she made on Sean's office door was erratic. Her knocks were rapid with half of them hitting air instead of the door.

"Come in."

She started speaking before she completely entered his office, and she even thought her speech was coffee infused. "Good morning, Sean. Yesterday, I was looking at the additional materials that went along with the Gordon Powell exhibit. I believe there is a story here, and I was wondering if I could do some research before you culled the piece."

Sean spoke as if he were an adult trying to rationalize a decision to a child with a *that's the way it is* answer. "The Board was very clear on the new direction. I'm sorry, but we are culling this exhibit."

She knew better than to say, *but why*; instead, she asked, "What are you going to do with this exhibit?"

A slight sigh escaped Sean's mouth. "Our asset assessment instrument rates this as low in recyclability. In this case, we are simply going to dispose of the materials."

"You can't just get rid of it. We generally check with the provider to see if they would like it returned."

Sean interrupted her before she could go any further. "The reason we have assessment instruments is to guide us in making appropriate decisions. This particular assessment instrument takes multiple variables into consideration: visual quality, appeal to modern audiences, fit with the other holdings and overall direction of the museum, marketability, impact on fund raising, and conditions set forth by the original provider. The Powell piece rated low on every indicator. Regarding the last criterion, the Kenyan museum that denotated it did so without conditions."

"Well, if you're just going to throw it away, may I have it?"

"If you wish," he answered resignedly.

That night, Sarah asked Wesley if he would come over and help her. They sat next to each other in Sarah's den with Wesley in front of the computer.

"So, I'm using my account to search this online database of old newspapers. We'll see what we can find on Gordon Powell," explained Wesley.

"Thank you so much for your help and for using your account. I don't have a subscription to that service."

"No problem at all. If you're this interested in something, the least I can do is help where I can and where I have expertise."

Sarah waited anxiously as Wesley spent the next few minutes searching on the computer.

"Ah. Found something."

Sarah almost jumped out of her seat. She leaned in to look at the screen, blocking Wesley's view. Wesley cleared his throat, and Sarah, realizing her impatience, moved back to her original spot. "Sorry. What is it?"

Wesley merely nodded and continued speaking. "This is an old newspaper article from 1919. I'll print it out, but I know you can't wait; so, I'll summarize it until you can fully read it yourself." Wesley scanned the article, summarizing as he scanned. "It says that Gordon and his family lived in Wyoming and then moved to Colorado. When his parents died suddenly, he and his younger brother, Grant, moved to Tennessee to live with their aunt. They hadn't been there long when

Gordon was drafted into World War I. Grant was underaged but ran off to join as well. Both were in the 30th Infantry Division, which was attached to the British Expeditionary Forces.   They fought in the Battle of Cambrai and in the Battle of the Selle. Grant was killed during this battle, and Gordon learned of it while the battle was still being waged. Gordon volunteered for a suicide mission to man the machine guns to allow the others to retreat. Gordon halted the German advance, but he was stranded behind enemy lines. For his heroism, Gordon was decorated with the French Croix de Guerre and the U.S. Distinguished Service Cross."

Although Sarah already knew all but the last part, she didn't want to dampen his enthusiasm or minimize his help. "That certainly explains his emotional suffering."

The next day, Sarah once again went to see Sean. Although she had been anxious ever since she arrived at work, she at least finished going over the list of exhibits to cull before approaching him. There was no sense in riling him by not finishing the task he had assigned her. She knocked on the frame of Sean's open door and walked inside. "I've completed reviewing the list, and everything is ok to cull." She knew that was the answer he was expecting, and she wondered why he even asked her to do the assignment if he already knew what he would cull. Although she knew his answer would be to double check if she asked him, she still thought it was a waste of time. But he could answer to the Board that the museum had done its due diligence in evaluating the museum holdings.

Sean nodded approvingly.

Sean seemed in a good mood, and Sarah hesitated briefly before blurting out what she had been preparing for all day. "Since there will be some down time for me anyway while the materials are culled, I wondered if I could use some of my vacation time. I have plenty built up. I would like to take some of my time to do some research on Gordon Powell."

"You have the time, and I'll approve two weeks. If you want to spend your vacation working, that's up to you. But I'll need you back after the two weeks to provide information on the new collections that are brought in."

Excitement exploded within Sarah, but she managed to calmly say, "Thank you, Sean." She didn't tell him that this would not be work for her; it was pure joy to get back to what she truly loved doing.

Sarah invited Wesley over to dinner at her place that night. Too excited to attempt cooking, she picked up takeout from one of Wesley's favorite restaurants. He would appreciate that more than her cooking. Plus, he was more used to eating restaurant food than eating home cooking anyway. She waited until Wesley had almost finished eating before she told him her news. "So, I told Sean that I wanted to take vacation to research this story. Do you want to come along? This could be a good story for you to report."

"You're going all the way to Africa, at least that's where I assume you are going, just to do research on this? This story really does mean a lot to you." Wesley paused a moment, and Sarah assumed he was considering her request to join him. "This is not the type of article our online magazine reports on. Besides, you know that I'm trying to get hired by a news organization like NPR, CNN, MSNBC, or one similar. In my last interview, I was told that if I could get a few more good articles, I would have a chance at getting hired. I'm working on one now. I'd love to go with you, but I can't afford to take the time."

"Will you miss me while I'm gone?"

Before Wesley could answer, his phone rang. He looked at the caller id and held up a finger. "Sorry. I have to take this." Wesley listened to the call. His only response was, "Thank you. I'd love to." He ended the call and looked at Sarah. "The magazine wants me to do another story as soon as I finish this one." Sarah wasn't sure what her facial expression said, but Wesley quickly added, "Yes. I will miss you." He leaned over to Sarah, and they shared a quick kiss.

Chapter 5

Sarah arrived at the Jomo Kenyatta International Airport in Nairobi, Kenya and rented a car. She had written down the address of the Kenyan museum from the cataloged information that Inez had provided. She found a parking space within a few blocks of the address and used her phone GPS to walk the short distance. When the phone indicated that she had arrived at her destination, she looked up at the building in front of her. She looked at her phone and back up at the building, bewildered. Although she was in a foreign city, she definitely felt like a lost tourist. Her thoughts raced and collided in her mind becoming an entangled ball of string she couldn't unravel. The sign on the building in front of her read *Nairobi Westlands School.* Her heart dropped as the disappointment set in and firmly gripped her. She could have kicked herself. Research 101 and common sense nipped at her mind telling her she should have done her homework before leaving home. With nothing left to lose, she entered the school and searched for the office.

Explaining her dilemma to the principal, she was directed to the school library. Her emotions were still a jumbled mess when she walked into the library and searched for the librarian. She found who she thought was the school librarian sitting behind a desk. As Sarah approached, the woman looked up and smiled. "Hello. May I help you?"

The pleasant voice put Sarah somewhat at ease. "I hope so. The principal said that you may have some information. This address is, or was, supposed to be for a museum, but it's obviously not."

The librarian was still pleasant, which made Sarah feel not quite as stupid as she had a moment earlier. "This school used to be a museum that was built in the 1950s, but it was dissolved in 1989. The building has served as a school since 1990. The old museum records are stored electronically though. I could look something up for you if you need information on a piece."

"That would be great." Sarah explained that she worked at a museum in the United States, and the materials they had on a particular exhibit came from the museum that used to be at this address. She showed the librarian the picture of Gordon Powell along with the catalog information. "I'm looking for information about the man in this photo. His name was Gordon Powell."

The woman looked down as she typed on the computer to begin the search. The librarian found the information almost immediately. "What materials the museum had were sent to the family at Powell's African Camp and Safari. I'll give you the address. The camp is still in existence at this address," the librarian replied with a wry smile. "The drive is several hours from here near the Serengeti National Park."

Sarah thanked the librarian for her help and left hopeful that what she was seeking was indeed at Powell's African Camp and

Safari.

🐘 🐘 🐘

Jack Powell and his twin sister, Jill ran Powell's African Camp and Safari. They were thirty-one years old, and both had light brown hair. Jack had a classic buzz cut. Jill had a part in her hair, slightly left of center, that framed her face and hung a few inches below her shoulders. Jack was five foot nine with a slight muscular build. Jill stood at five foot five with a slender build. Jack had been enjoying his usual morning cup of Kenyan coffee before he and Jill had gotten into the same ongoing argument they had been having regularly for the past several months.

"Even with full bookings, our financial outlook hasn't picked up yet. We haven't put a dent in our loan principal; we're barely paying the interest. At this rate, I don't see how we can keep Powell's African Camp and Safari going much longer." Jack leaned back against the jeep he was standing by, took a gulp of coffee and waited for Jill's response. He knew it was coming; it was only delayed by Jill tightly closing her eyes and massaging her temples with her thumb and middle finger. He knew the look. Being twins, both could generally read the other's nonverbal cues and could anticipate what the other was going to say. Although Jill was too polite to say it, he knew she was thinking, *I can't believe I'm about to repeat the same thing again.*

"Why don't you want to try some of the ideas that Gacoki and I have?"

"That takes money."

"Not that much?"

Now it was Jack's turn to squeeze his eyes shut and rub his temples. "Even if we did implement them, they wouldn't bring in that much revenue for us. Most would go to third parties or for employee costs. Besides, with the consistent full bookings we have, we can't handle additional guests."

"Well, can we expand any?"

"The bank won't give us an additional loan. Both of us have tried on separate occasions. Even if they did give us a loan, I don't see how we could afford to pay off two loans. We can barely afford the one we have."

"We have to try something!"

Jack's frustration was beginning to get the best of him. "It's time to take our guests on the safari. We're not solving anything here anyway."

"This is why we keep having the same argument. Every time we get to this point, you walk away."

The long drive after an even longer flight was grueling. Sleepiness, like gravity, tugged relentlessly at her head. Like Sisyphus pushing the boulder up the hill, she would hold her head up only for it to begin drifting downward again. Sarah almost pulled on the side of the road to take a catnap when she noticed that she was only a few miles from her destination. She shook her head, tapped her hands on the steering wheel, and hummed aloud to push herself the final few miles. The relief at the end of a long journey was like a shot of adrenaline that at last energized her. She didn't know if exhaustion or bad luck was the culprit behind her befuddlement when the GPS on her phone alerted her that she had arrived at her destination. Just like at the school that was supposed to be a museum, what was supposed to be the camp was an open gate and a dirt road. She didn't see any signs, and the dirt road could have led anywhere. Feeling as though she had nothing left to lose, she decided to take the dirt road. Hopefully, it would lead to the camp. If it didn't, she would be taking more than a catnap in her rental car.

Sarah had been on much worse dirt roads, roads with potholes that reminded her of scenes of the moon or roads with such high ridges in the middle that you had to line the tires of the car with the ridge or suffer scraping the underbelly of your car. This dirt road had none of those obstacles, but it was nonetheless a bumpy ride with what seemed to be miniature speed bumps at regular intervals. Suddenly, the car began vibrating more than it had been over the bumps. Then, it began vibrating a lot. She wondered why the car was vibrating so much until the realization sunk in that she must have a flat tire. Frustration mixed with anger slammed into her like a battering ram. Although Sarah wasn't prone to cursing, several choice words escaped her mouth like the sweat that poured from her body. She stopped the car and lowered the window letting the remaining curse words escape into the hot air. Looking ahead and then behind in her rearview mirror, she didn't see a vehicle in sight.

She had never changed a tire before, but she had seen it done several times. Surely, she could copy the steps, especially since she couldn't call AAA. She opened the door and froze. Staring back at her was a lion. She had seen lions from a safe distance in zoos but seeing one that could actually get to her sent chills up her spine, paralyzing her. She willed herself to take control of her muscles and she slowly and quietly closed the car door. Uncertain of what to do, she sat in the car hoping it would leave, but even if it did, the thought of getting out and changing the tire was like a horror movie where the monster could reappear seemingly out of thin air.

Something charged by her car and every muscle in her body was once again paralyzed. When she saw that what went by her was a jeep, she tried to relax, but the tension caused her muscles to ache as though she were a novice who had just completed a triathlon. Once the jeep stopped just ahead of her, the lion sauntered off. The man who got out of the jeep wore a shirt with some emblem on it that she couldn't make out at this distance. He approached her car and tapped on the window. Sarah rolled down the window to greet her salvation, "Oh, thank heaven …" He cut her off before she could finish. Instead of being a harbinger of hope he seemed more a denouncing demon.

"This is a private road. What are you doing here? Didn't you see the gate and the sign?"

Sarah was taken aback. "I didn't see a sign."

The corners of his mouth turned down into a frown, but before he could say anything else, a call came through on his two-way radio.

"Jack, come in."

The man took his two-way radio from his side belt. "This is Jack.

Go ahead."

"The gate to the private road was left open."

Jack looked to Sarah who went wide-eyed with an *I told you so* look of self-satisfaction. Jack turned his attention back to the radio. "Go ahead and close it. I'll remind everyone to keep the gate closed. Oh, do you see the sign that says Private Road." This time Jack looked at Sarah and gave a wry smile. Sarah figured that was Jack's *I gotcha* look. The voice on the other end of the radio went silent for a good fifteen seconds.

"Barely," came the reply on the other end. "It's almost covered up. I wouldn't have seen it if I didn't know where to look. I'll cut back the growth."

"Copy. Out."

Sarah returned the previous look she had given, and Jack huffed. "See! I was telling truth."

Jack relented. "I'll ask someone to change the tire for you and bring the vehicle back to camp. Leave the keys in the car and don't lock the door."

Without thinking, Sarah asked, "Is it safe to just leave the keys in the car?"

Jack's eyebrows rose. "Are you afraid an elephant is going to take your car for a joy ride?"

"Well, its trunk would make a good jack, but I don't think the elephant would fit in my car."

"Just climb in the jeep, and let's go."

Apparently, Jack didn't have much of a sense of humor, thought Sarah. She thought the response was quick-witted herself. Sarah climbed into the back of the jeep to face the stares of half a dozen or more people. She held out her arms, palms facing up. "Sorry."

One man replied, "Oh, no need to apologize. It was quite entertaining."

Embarrassed, Sarah tried to avoid eye contact with everyone on the ride back. She was glad that the jeep handled the bumpy road much better than her car did. Still, even as tired as she was, the ride was definitely not going to put her to sleep. Once the jeep arrived back at camp, Sarah waited until everyone else exited before she got out.

Jack walked over to Sarah; his face showed little emotion. "We're supposed to pick up camp guests. It's all in the literature."

Having not won the previous argument, Sarah thought that he was trying a different angle this time. "Oh, I'm not a guest."

Jack put his hands on his hips and gave some sort of barely audible grunt. His mouth formed a hard line, and his forehead furrowed. Sarah knew she didn't want to hear what was about to come out of Jack's mouth.

"What?" he questioned sharply. "It will be night soon. Where do you expect to spend the night?"

Unprepared again. Sarah hadn't even considered that. She made a mental note that if she were ever to do field research again, she really needed to plan ahead. She didn't want to irritate Jack further; so, she tried to respond in as pleasant a voice as she could muster. "Well, I do need a place to spend the night. Do you know of somewhere nearby?"

Apparently, her voice wasn't pleasant enough. Jack's eyes widened, and one corner of his mouth turned up. He threw up his hands and turned to walk away. He pointed to the wide-open space. With his back still turned, he finally answered. "Pick a spot, but I wouldn't go near the watering hole. It might be a little crowded in the morning." With that, Jack walked off.

Shivers went through Sarah at the thought of spending the night in the open in the African wild, and she quickly ran to catch up to him. As Sarah tried to engage him in conversation, he continued walking. "I'm looking for Jack Powell. I was told by the school in Nairobi, which used to be a museum, that he was here."

"Lady."

Sarah could sense the irritation in Jack's voice. "It's Sarah … Well, not Lady Sarah, just Sarah."

"I'm busy. I have things to do before I turn in. Since our accommodations are full, and you haven't paid, I'll set up a pup tent for you tonight. You can eat here. In the morning, your car will be here, and you can leave."

Sarah stopped in her tracks as Jack continued walking away. Once he got about ten feet away, Sarah said the first thing that came into her mind. "You're kidding about the pup tent, right?"

Jack stopped and let out a sigh. "I suppose so. I can let you sleep in the social tent. I'll cordon off a section. Oh, tents for paying guests have en suite bathrooms. Since the social tent doesn't have an inside bathroom, I'll leave a two-way radio with you. If you need to use the bathroom, call, and we'll escort you to the bathroom."

In the dining tent, Sarah set with the man in the jeep, who commented that he was entertained by the exchange between Jack and Sarah, along with his wife. They had been at the camp a few days and were thoroughly enjoying it. They were probably in their fifties, and this was their first trip to Africa. When she found out that they were from Tennessee, she couldn't help but ask if they had ever heard of Gordon Powell. Although hearing about a World War I hero who had barely lived in the state was very unlikely, she wanted to pursue every opportunity that presented itself to her. As she suspected, they had not. They didn't even link the last name of *Powell* to the camp where they were vacationing. Still, she had a good conversation with the couple, and it had taken her mind off both the arduous journey to get here as well as the embarrassment she had suffered several times today.

As promised, Jack had sectioned off a section of the social tent and had put up a curtained privacy barrier around it. She was completely exhausted by nine o'clock, and her head begged to hit the pillow. The social tent was open for activities and camaraderie until eleven o'clock or even midnight. The sounds of metal-tipped darts thudding against a dartboard, ice clanging against a shaker as cocktails were mixed, glasses clinked in cheers, the crack of billiard balls the low hummed chatter of the guests, and the occasional belly laugh recreated the luxurious indulgence of the 1920s African safari camps.

The sounds mixed together and faded in the background, creating a safety net around her, and soon, she was in a peaceful sleep.

The fuzzy headedness one experiences when waking from a well-deserved rest from a weary mind and a fatigued body caused immense confusion for Sarah when she awoke in the dark. The only thing she knew for certain was that she needed to pee desperately. When her feet hit the floor, something seemed off. The height of the bed didn't feel right. She reached for her nightstand, but it wasn't there. Where was she, she wondered? Still feeling tired, her body swayed, and she almost stumbled back into the bed. As her eyes slowly adjusted to the darkness, her surroundings didn't seem familiar. After a few seconds of anxiety, she finally realized that she wasn't back home in Colorado but rather a camp in Kenya. She wondered what time it was, but her phone was nowhere to be found at the moment. The time didn't really matter though. Whether it was one a.m. or six a.m., she had to pee.

Her eyes caught sight of the two-way radio, Jack had left for her, but who knew how long that would take for someone to come. If it were Jack, and he knew she needed to pee, he might take an extra five minutes beyond the normal time it would take for someone to get to her. She looked down and noticed she was wearing her favorite camouflage pajamas. She didn't even remember putting them on, much less where the rest of her clothes were. At least her shoes were nearby. Was it worth the gamble to go out on her own? Butterflies flew around in her stomach as she debated whether or not to use the two-way radio. If she were quick, no one would know the difference. The devil on her shoulder finally won the argument, and she decided to go quickly outside, pee, and return, no one the wiser.

Sarah could hear the swishing noise her pajamas made against the tall grass. If she could hear it, what else could? She was having second thoughts now about listening to the devil on her shoulder. Finding several shrubs, Sarah thought she had ventured far enough. The shrubs were low-lying, and Sarah had to squat low to the ground. Oh God, she thought. I hope there are no snakes out here. How would she explain a snakebite on her butt? Wasn't Africa home to the black mamba snake, one of the most poisonous snakes in the world? Where was the nearest medical facility? Her heart began to beat quickly; she could almost feel it hitting the inside of her chest. She was wide awake at this point. As these questions were going through her mind and causing her body to go into survival mode, she heard the brushing of grass not ten feet away as well as a noise like the breaking of a small stick. Did she see movement as well? Involuntarily, a piercing scream erupted from her causing her own eardrums to vibrate, and she ran for a tree. A voice in her mind told her to run serpentine, and another voice told her to run in a direct route. The conflicting voices caused her to do some of both. Reaching the tree, she jumped to the first limb and climbed until she could go no further. Her heart was beating so fast that everything around her began to spin. She was light-headed and breathing quick shallow breaths. Her palms were sweaty, and her grip on the tree loosened. Her consciousness was leaving her body. Oh God, she was going to fall.

"Hey!"

The shout below her shook her out of her panic. For some odd reason, rather than frightening her further, it had a comforting effect. Her shallow breathing stopped immediately, and she gulped a lungful of air. Awareness jolted her brain. She could see flashlights and lanterns and people stirring outside of their tents. Jack was beneath the tree with a rifle looking up at her, sighing and shaking his head. Jack was the one who had kept her from falling out of the tree with just one word.

"You had to go the bathroom, didn't you?" Not waiting for her response, he continued, "Didn't I tell you to call, and someone would escort you?"

Shame surged through her. Why had she not listened to the angel on her shoulder? She was embarrassed again. She had experienced more embarrassment within a twenty-four-hour period than she had in the past year. "I didn't want to bother you."

For the first time since she had met him, Jack laughed. "Well, thank you for not bothering me. I have this habit every night after midnight to run outside with a rifle!"

Was Jack having fun at her expense, or was he masking anger or worry? She couldn't tell. Whatever his emotion was, she needed to apologize. "I'm sorry. I heard a noise." As soon as the last sentence escaped her mouth, she regretted it. She just added more fodder for Jack. Why hadn't she just stopped at *I'm sorry*?

"Really? In the middle of the African wilderness, you heard a noise at night. That never happens."

Now, Sarah felt she had to explain her actions. "I thought it might have been a tiger." Even in the dark and from her distance from Jack, she could see a tiny smirk on his face.

"Well, that would have been a sight for sure seeing as there are no tigers in Africa, unless one happened to come over from India on vacation."

Sarah bristled at the comment. Any fear was now gone, replaced by a growing anger and need for explanation.

Jack yelled out to the onlookers. "Everything is fine. Please, don't worry, and go back to bed."

"Well maybe a lion. I assume there are lions in Africa," she remarked with deprecation.

Jack looked at her with a blank face. Perhaps she had stung him with the surliness of her comment. "There are, but if it had actually been a lion, and it wanted to eat you, it would have caught you before you ever made it to the tree. Are you able to climb down? Let me help you."

Sarah descended the tree, taking more caution than she did on the climb up. She grabbed Jack's sturdy hand and immediately felt comfort. Any lingering animosity seemed to evaporate.

"What are you wearing?" he asked. "Are those camouflage pajamas?" He chuckled. "Well, a lion would have never spotted you in those."

The bitterness that was evaporating fell down like rain, and Sarah once again felt the heat rising within her. "I can get down by myself. Thank you very much."

Jack let go of her hand. She climbed down the short, remaining distance to the ground and stumbled as her last foot hit the ground.

"I'll escort you to the bathroom."

One corner of Sarah's mouth rose as she looked at him.

"Don't worry. It's private. Besides," he replied with a smile, "you'll blend in anyway with your pajamas."

Chapter 6

The next morning, Sarah was up and dressed, early. She straightened up and moved the privacy curtain to the side. As she was finishing, Jill entered the social tent.

"Good morning! You must be Sarah. I'm Jack's sister. I didn't get to meet you last night."

At the mention of Jack's name, Sarah thought about how impolite he had been, and she verbalized it before thinking. "If you're anything like your brother, I could only take one of you at a time." What did she just say? Sarah couldn't believe she had just made such a rude comment to someone she just met. "I'm sorry. That was very rude of me. Please forgive me. I just didn't hit it off too well yesterday with Jack."

"No offense taken. I'm sorry about my brother. He can come across as pretty stern sometimes, but he really is just a teddy bear at heart."

Sarah tried to make a joke out of the comment Jill had just made.

"I don't think there are any bears in Africa, teddy or otherwise." Was that supposed to be funny, she thought to herself? Jill smiled. It was a quick smile accompanied by a slight chuckle all with her lips still together.

Probably a nervous smile, thought Sarah.

"He must have been exceptionally rude. I'm Jill by the way."

"It's a pleasure to meet you, Jill. Wait! Your parents actually named you Jack and Jill?" Sarah could have kicked herself for that comment as well. The only thing she could do was just apologize. "Again, I'm sorry. That was also very rude of me. I'm usually not like this. Really. I suppose I'm tired from traveling and from not sleeping well last night. I'm not trying to excuse my behavior, just explain it. I promise that I will do my best to not make any more stupid or insensitive comments."

Jill fully laughed this time. Sarah was glad that she could take it on the chin.

"No problem. I understand completely. It actually happens quite a bit. A lot of our guests are tired and ill when they arrive. It takes a lot of travel time for most people to get here, but they are completely at ease after a day or so here. Jack had a tough day yesterday; I'm sure you'll find he is a different person today. He really is a nice guy once you get to know him, and that means a lot coming from a sister."

Jack walked into the social tent as Jill was finishing speaking. "Good morning. It's Ms. Jacobs, isn't it?"

Perhaps Jill was right. Jack did seem to be a different person this morning, so far. "Yes, but please call me Sarah."

Simultaneously, both Jack and Sarah apologized. "I'm sorry about yesterday." Both laughed.

"I see you've met my sister, Jill. I'm sure she said something about me. I know I can be a bear sometimes."

Sarah raised her head and eyebrows and rubbed her chin as she spoke deliberately. "So, there are bears in Kenya," she replied in such a way that her comment was somewhere between a statement and a question.

"Just one," smiled Jack. Afterwards, Jack crossed his arms and looked earnestly into Sarah's eyes. "So, what did you come all this way to see me about?"

Sarah's heart skipped a beat at the thought that she might get some real answers to some of her questions. "My degree is in cultural anthropology, but I work at a museum in Colorado, which doesn't call for a degree in cultural anthropology very often." A few people told Sarah that when she got really excited about something that she rambled like a giddy six-year-old, and she had caught herself doing just that. Jack's mouth was trying to maintain a straight line, but it quivered as if wanting to break into a smile. "I'm rambling. Anyway, the museum was going to cull an exhibit, but I have a hunch there's an interesting story behind it."

Sarah grabbed her portfolio and pulled out a picture, letter, newspaper article, and the pages torn from the diary. Jack and Jill stood beside each other so that they could see the materials that Sarah had brought. Sarah held up the picture first. "This picture is of a

World War I veteran named Gordon Powell. From the picture, he appears to be a hunter."

Jill furrowed her brow. "What's the connection to the museum?"

"He lived in Colorado at one time," answered Sarah.

Jack let out a single laugh through his nose. It sounded almost like he was blowing his nose. "It must not take much to get an exhibit in your museum."

Sarah wasn't expecting this type of response. If one of her ancestors had a museum exhibit, she would have been proud and certainly more curious, and the thought of someone wanting to remove it from the museum would definitely get a rise out of her.

"Why are they getting rid of it now?" asked Jill.

Even though Jill asked why it was being removed, her attitude seemed similar to Jack's. It was just a question asked nonchalantly to make conversation. What was with these people? "The museum is changing its focus. The materials on Gordon Powell were given to our museum back in the sixties from the Kenyan museum. When I visited the Kenyan museum, it had been turned into a school. The materials they had about Gordon Powell were sent here in 1989. I know it's a long shot, but do you have those materials?" Sarah looked expectantly from one to the other.

Jack and Jill looked wide-eyed at each other, and their mouths hung open slightly. Jack served as the spokesperson. "They would have been sent to our parents, but I doubt we still have them. If we do, there is only one place they would be. I'll take you there, and we can look to see if we can find anything. It's pretty cluttered, and finding something may be difficult." Jack hesitated and looked questioningly at Jill. He seemed as though he wasn't sure whether to say the next part or not. "I have to be honest with you. I don't know much about Gordon Powell, only that he was a great, great, I don't know how many greats grandfather. I was told he was a hunter, which is the exact opposite of what we do here; so, I don't have a lot of warm feelings regarding him. His kind tried and still tries to ruin Africa."

That explained the lack of curiosity and lack of pride, thought Sarah. They were ashamed of him. If the family wasn't interested in helping her, she didn't stand much of a chance of finding out more. Jack, of course, pledged help, but was he just being cordial? Did he really mean it? She needed to find a way to get both brother and sister interested in wanting to find out more, but she wasn't sure at this moment exactly how to accomplish that feat. The hunting part seemed to be the biggest turn-off for Jack. Her spirits brightened when she remembered the letter. Perhaps that would change his mind about his ancestor. "Based on this letter, that may not be the case."

"Maybe so, but I expect that it will take more than a letter to convince me."

Sarah was now determined she needed to change Jack's opinion. "Well, let me show both of you what I have." Jack and Jill gathered beside each other as Sarah prepared to show them the letter. "This newspaper article says that during World War I, Gordon volunteered for a suicide mission when he learned that his younger brother was killed in battle. Gordon ended up surviving and was decorated as a war hero. Looking at this letter he wrote, he must have suffered from PTSD and was depressed to the point that he took up hunting man-eaters because he didn't care if he lived or not. When he met this English aristocrat, everything changed. Gordon was killed in 1950 while saving the very rhino that gored him. He stopped a hunter from shooting it. So, you see, nothing suggests that Gordon ever trophy hunted or hunted for sport. Like you and Jill, he tried to save wildlife. I'd love to find out the whole story."

The inside corners of Jack's eyebrows rose. "That's news to me."

"Me too," added Jill. Jill's whole body was tense, almost as if she had vividly pictured the scenes that Sarah described.

At least Jack and Jill seemed more engaged after hearing the information, thought Sarah. She hoped they would be more convinced to help her or to identify other leads she could explore.

"Jill and I will be happy to help you as best we can." Jack paused and darted his eyes to Jill. Some secret seemed to pass between the twin brother and sister. Jack began hesitantly, "Look, I want to make up for the way I behaved yesterday. Although people say that I can be a little edgy at times, I really wasn't myself yesterday. I want to apologize for my rude behavior. We've had a cancellation for a week that starts today, and I would very much appreciate it if you stayed. Call it a truce. You don't have to pay anything. I'll show you the sights and what the camp is all about, if you like, and the rest of the time, you can continue with your research, if we can indeed find anything. Do we have a deal?"

As Jack held out his hand to shake on the deal, Sarah looked into his eyes. She didn't think she could describe honest eyes, but Jack's eyes were what she pictured, if she had to pick out a pair of honest eyes from a lineup. He certainly seemed sincere, especially if he were letting her stay for free. And it seemed as though they truly were going to help her. She couldn't think of a better outcome. Well, she could think of a better outcome … actually finding the whole story. But in the meantime, this was the best deal there was. Sarah extended her hand and matched Jack's firm grip. "Deal!" she said as they shook hands.

Jack had all of Sarah's belongings moved to her new tent, and one of the camp workers had changed the tire on her rental car and brought it to camp. Her new tent was much better than the small space she had in the social tent. The first thing she did was check out the en suite bathroom. No more going outside at night to pee. Sometimes the simple joys were the best. As she took a self-guided tour of her tent, she could certainly see the appeal of the camp's 1920s décor. Some of the pieces actually looked to be restored 1920s originals. Others were probably 1920s-style replicas. The opulent living and social quarters provided a sense of safety in the middle of the wilderness. She could see how some would take it as an overt symbol of colonialism, but Sarah saw it as an opportunity for education. She believed that the best way to educate people was to provide an engaging and immersive experience in a culture. Seeing how cultures clashed helped bring about understanding. She believed herself to also be a realist. To bring people in, one couldn't expect a person to just decide out of the blue that they wanted to find out about a culture. Old movies and books painted a picture of Africa in the late nineteenth and early twentieth century as a place of danger and romance. Something like this camp had to be created to draw people in, especially those from Western cultures. What better way to draw people in than to entice people's imagination of a carefree bygone era? This had to be done within reason, of course, a careful balance that wouldn't offend the very people that one wanted others to understand.

Sarah had not called her boyfriend, Wesley, since she had arrived in Africa. He would probably be worried about her. From Jack, she heard that the best place to get a signal was behind the social tent. It wasn't until Wesley answered the phone that Sarah realized the time difference.

"Hi, Sarah. I wondered when I was going to hear from you."

"I'm sorry to call so late. What is it, like eleven p.m. there?" Sarah cringed when she heard her voice state the time.

"No problem. I'm just glad you called. How is everything? Are you ok?"

"I'm fine, just a lot of mishaps, but I can tell you about most of them later. I wanted to let you know that the Kenyan museum no longer exists. It's a school, and I felt stupid for not checking it out before I left. But I have a lead now. I'm at Powell's African Camp and Safari near the Serengeti National Park."

"Wow! Sounds like you're having quite an adventure. Isn't that the camp where your grandfather was?"

"It is, but it looks a lot different from the pictures. They must have done a lot of updating."

"I'm sure. The picture of your grandfather had to have been taken a long time ago."

"How is your article coming along?"

"I finished the one I was working on and have started the one I accepted from the phone call I received when I was at your house."

"Well, I won't keep you. I just wanted to let you know I made it here safely."

"I'm glad you did. It's nice hearing your voice. I imagine the cell phone service there is not great; so, let me tell you something while you still have reception. Just so you'll know I've been thinking about you while you've been gone, I did some more digging, and I sent you what I found. Check your Dropbox. Be careful out there and call me when you can."

"I will. Bye."

Jack walked up as Sarah put away her phone. "Did you get through?"

"Yes. Thank you for letting me know this was the best place to get a signal."

"Glad to help. I wouldn't want your boyfriend thinking something terrible happened to you, like getting eaten by a tiger."

Jack's beaming eyes told Sarah he was joking. She liked this side of Jack. As Jill said, he must have just had a bad day yesterday. "My boyfriend is a journalist, and he found some information that he sent me."

"That's great. Maybe we can start piecing the puzzle together for you. Would you like to see if we can find the museum materials?"

"Definitely. I'm ready. Let's go!"

Jack took her to the staff lodge, as he called it. This was a wooden structure, not a canvas tent like most of the other structures in the camp. It didn't appear to be very big from the outside and certainly didn't bring the image to mind of what she would call a lodge. She wondered why Jack didn't have her stay in the lodge last night rather than a small section of the social tent. She dismissed the thought quickly. She reasoned that if financial information or other day-to-day information was there, she would have done the same thing for a person she didn't know who showed up out of the blue. They entered into a small foyer. A staircase was along the left-side, perhaps to some bedrooms upstairs. The office was the first room on the right. They kept walking and entered a storeroom. Inside was another door leading to what was perhaps a bathroom. Near the back of the storeroom was another staircase that led down. Jack flipped on a light, and they descended the stairs into a basement. There were no windows in the basement and the smell of staleness hung in the air like a fog that refused to dissipate. The basement was packed full of filing cabinets, boxes, and shelving units. There was no order to anything. It reminded Sarah of an extremely large garage that someone used as storage for anything and everything. If Sarah had been prone to claustrophobia, she would have already gone back upstairs. She had seen television shows about hoarders, and this looked exactly like the images she had seen on television. Where would one even start in all this mess? A mouse would have had trouble navigating the maze of narrow walkways. In fact, it appeared as though every one of them dead ended. "Wow! You said it was cluttered, but I didn't realize it would be this cluttered. You could use the services of our archivist, Inez."

Jack didn't seem upset by her comment. "There's a reason it's this way, but that story is probably not as interesting as the one you're exploring," he remarked matter-of-factly. "We have a computer and printer down here, if you need them for any reason. You mentioned your boyfriend sent you some information. If you want to go ahead and print that out, please feel to do so. It might help to have all the information you currently have before you begin searching."

Sarah took out her phone and found the document that Wesley sent. She added the printer to her settings and sent the document to the printer. Jack stumbled to the printer, knocking a few boxes over in the process. As he retrieved the printout, Jill walked in. He handed the printout to Sarah and moved several boxes out of the way revealing three hidden chairs behind them. He pulled them out into the small space he had just cleared and patted the seat of one of the chairs, indicating for everyone to take a seat. Sarah sat in the middle chair, but she doubted that Jack or Jill could see what she had.

"This is another old newspaper article." Sarah summarized the article as she read. "After Gordon was stranded behind enemy lines, he came across an African soldier, name Kagiso, who was in the British Expeditionary Forces. Kagiso's friend, Chima, had been killed, and Kagiso almost shot Gordon when he approached. They headed out together toward the allied lines. Eventually, they came across a group of German soldiers. One German soldier was about to use his bayonet to stab a British officer. Both groups opened fire. Although Gordon and Kagiso suffered injuries, they were able to save the British officer. All three made it back to the allied lines and were taken to a field hospital. The British soldier was Viscount Anthony Montagu, and his father was the Earl of Halifax."

"That's interesting. I never heard that story," remarked Jack.

"Did you ever figure out how you were related go Gordon Powell?" asked Sarah.

Jack shot a glance around Sarah to Jill, as if looking for permission to reply. "Yes. Jill and I talked about it while you ate breakfast and called your boyfriend. He was our great grandfather."

Sarah turned her attention back to the article. "I wonder what happened after the war?"

"If there is an answer, it may be in one of these boxes."

Sarah had been curious about something for a while. It had been nagging at her, but she didn't want to ask for fear of upsetting Jack. Now that they seemed to be on steadier ground, her curiosity won over, and she risked asking the question. "Do you know why you don't know much about your great-grandfather, Gordon Powell?" Jack hesitated. His shoulders stopped and tensed in mid-breath, and Sarah wondered if she had made a mistake in asking.

"Our grandfather and parents were killed in a jeep accident when we were thirteen. If they told us, the information either didn't stick with us or we were too young to care."

"I'm so sorry to hear that." Sarah was unsure what to say next, mentally rejecting numerous potential responses. Finally, she remarked, "In my experience, younger people aren't that interested in genealogy. People generally don't become interested in their heritage until they are older." Sarah regretted the comment as soon as she had made it. Rather than showing sympathy, she sounded like an academician. She quickly added, "I didn't mean to sound callous with my last comment. I truly am sorry for your loss."

"No apologies are necessary," replied Jill. "It was a long time ago, and what you said is probably generally true. I wish I did know more about our family history."

The dimple formed by Jill's half smile only served to reinforce Sarah's regret of making the comment.

The silence was palpable and uncomfortable until Jack finally spoke. "Well, daylight is burning as the saying goes, and these boxes aren't going to go through themselves. We might as well get started."

"I need to head back to our guests," remarked Jill. "I hope you two don't mind going through these without me, but I promise to help later."

"We've got this," replied Jack.

Several hours had passed, and Jack and Sarah had already gone through about a third of the boxes. They marked the ones they had gone through and had moved enough boxes out of the way to put the stack of reviewed boxes, which formed their own mountain.

Sarah's face hair was flushed from the stale, stagnant air, and her hair was tousled and covered with a thin film of dust. "I haven't found anything." Her glum voice was raspy from the dust she had inhaled. "Have you?"

Jack responded with an equally downcast voice. "The only thing I've found is that I can get rid of most of these boxes. I've marked the ones to keep with a different color."

"I'm sorry I couldn't do the same, but I don't know what you need to keep." Sarah was ready to concede for the time being and was relieved when Jack felt the same.

"I've had enough for a while," he responded wearily. His sleeves were rolled up, and Sarah could see the film of dust covering his arms from where she was standing. Jack ran his hand through his disheveled hair and wiped the sweat from his face. "Let's take a break and go through more later."

"Does all work and no play make Jack a dull boy?"

"Perhaps, but it also makes Sarah a dull girl! You can't come to Africa and spend the whole time in a basement with stale-smelling, dust-covered boxes. Let me take you on an outing?"

"I could certainly go for an outing right about now. Where are we going?"

"It's a surprise but wear something that you can get wet."

"How wet?

"Very wet."

Sarah went back to her tent to change. She didn't realize just how disheveled she looked until she saw her reflection in the mirror. She didn't even want to be seen by wildlife, looking the way she did at the moment. She wanted to take a shower, but Jack said she would get wet; so, taking a shower would probably be pointless. Still, she didn't want to be seen the way she was. She grabbed a nearby cloth, wet it, and wiped away the layers of dust and the beads of sweat that clung to her like clothes. The course fabric of the cloth grazed her skin, rubbing away the grime, returning her skin to its normal color and providing a refreshing coolness. The aroma of some natural perfume the camp provided dissolved the stale, musty scent that had permeated her body. Next, she ran a comb through her tangled nest-like hair. Each stroke chased away more dust. Using her brush, she tidied the unruliness of her hair into some semblance of order. A change of clothes shed the weary look about her and left her feeling refreshed.

As Sarah walked outside of her tent, she took a deep breath of fresh air and exhaled slowly, driving away any remaining staleness that had settled in her lungs. She heard Jill's voice, along with a man's drifting her way over the slight breeze in the air. The voices were music compared to the scrapping of cardboard and the thudding of moved boxes in the basement. When Sarah reached the source of the voices, Jill looked up.

"Hi, Sarah. Did you find what you were looking for?"

"Not yet." The thought of all of those boxes with nothing to show for it was enough to dampen her spirit. But the thought of just one of the boxes containing the treasure she was searching for helped sustain her. "Jack and I went through a lot of boxes. Jack said that since I came to Africa, I needed to do more than look through old boxes."

The man standing next to Jill beamed a toothy smile. "Jack is smarter than I thought!"

Sarah wondered who the dark-skinned man was. She must have sent the thought telepathically to Jill because Jill immediately sprang alert as if remembering her manners. "Sarah, this is Gacoki. He works here at the camp. He was born and raised in a nearby village."

"Pleased to meet you, Gacoki."

"And you as well." The toothy grin reappeared, and Gacoki reached out to shake Sarah's hand.

Jill glanced from Sarah to Gacoki. "I've told Gacoki about your research into Gordon Powell." Jill shriveled her shoulders as if she were a kid with her hand caught in the cookie jar by her parent. "I hope you don't mind."

"Not at all." Sarah turned to face Gacoki directly. "Do you know anything about Gordon Powell?" Sarah knew it seemed crazy to ask everyone she met if they knew anything about Gordon Powell, but she wanted to make sure she exhausted all options. Sometimes it was a small world, and one never knew the connections that others might have with someone.

Gacoki's smile faded as he grew serious. "Not really, but my grandfather might. I can ask him if you'd like."

Sarah gave a slight sigh of thankfulness. "That would be wonderful. Thank you."

Jill raised her head as if she were looking for something or someone, and her eyes darted quickly around the area. She instinctively lowered her voice. "I hope you didn't overhear us when you walked up."

Sarah wondered what secrets had passed between the two, and she suddenly felt as though she had intruded on an intimate moment or a private conversation. Sarah's voice wavered. "No. I'm sorry. I didn't mean to interrupt."

Jill's eyes sparkled, probably in reaction to Sarah's apparent guilt, Sarah thought. "You didn't interrupt. Gacoki and I were just talking about our ideas for the camp again. Jack wants to keep everything as it is though."

Sarah sighed in relief over not hearing some treasured secret. She had not realized that her shoulders had tensed until she felt them relax into place. "I promise not to tell," she replied in a whispered voice.

"Promise not to tell what?"

Jack's voice, suddenly beside her, sent electricity surging throughout her body, and her body tensed. Like one of the predators in the savanna, Jack had silently and stealthily skulked into her vicinity. By the look of surprise on Jill's face, she was apparently as caught off guard as Sarah was by Jack's silent approach. The feeling of guilt quickly put her on the defensive, but she was able to turn her response into a playful jab. "That you were nice to me today. They thought it might ruin your image."

Jack looked mildly affronted. "I'm nice all the time." The rise in tenor in his voice betrayed his own confidence, and Jill and Gacoki burst into simultaneous laughter. A look of acquiescence settled on Jack's face. "I'm not going to let your fun at my expense ruin my demeanor." A look of stoicism entered his eyes as his and Jill's eyes met.

As Jack turned to Sarah, she saw the stoicism fade as it was replaced by a warm glow that made her tingle inside. She quickly squelched the tingle, reminding herself that she had a boyfriend and that she was here on business.

"Are you ready to go, Sarah?"

"Ready."

They walked along a trail that had been worn away leaving only the barest trace of grass. The worn trail was narrow, and the constant swishing sound of grass against legs accompanied them the entire way. Sarah could hear the sound before the view came into sight. The sound of the water, like a constant muffled thunder, carried over the breeze and combined with the sound of rustling grass to produce a song that only nature could sing. At first, the sounds blended harmoniously, but as they got closer, the sound of cascading water grew louder until it overpowered the sound of the bowing grass. As they rounded a bend in the trail, Sarah saw the waterfall. "This is gorgeous," bubbled Sarah.

Jack tied his backpack to a limb on an acacia tree. He took off his boots and stripped down to a bathing suit. The tingling that Sarah felt earlier returned as she saw Jack's muscular and hairy chest. Jack looked over to Sarah with a look that Sarah interpreted as, *here's the part where we get wet.* Sarah mimicked Jack and was soon brandishing her own bathing suit. Wesley would have laughed if he had seen her pack a bathing suit. This was supposed to be a research trip. At least she had been prepared with her clothes even if she had lacked preparation in other areas. She always did overpack, but in times such as this one, overpacking came in handy. Jack folded their clothes, put them in something similar to a duffle bag and tied it onto the acacia limb as well.

"I don't see any ants, but it doesn't pay to take chances," remarked Jack.

They walked toward the pool across some rocks. Jack helped her as her tender feet danced from the heat and hardness of the rocks. Sarah lost her balance at one point and grabbed for balance at a lone acacia tree that was growing between two rocks. Once they reached the end of the rocks, a sandy beach jettied into the water. Sarah's feet sank into the spongy sand, and water sprung up, enveloping her toes. As her feet sank a little further, the water hugged her ankles, its coolness sending a shiver up her spine. Jack quickly made his way into chest-deep water, turned, and motioned for Sarah to join him. Sarah was sweating from the heat of the walk, and Sarah's anticipation of the embrace of the cool water urged her forward. When the water was up to her knees, she saw the bottom make a sudden drop. She looked around deciding whether or not to take the sudden plunge, as Jack had. The sun's rays shimmered along the surface of the water, and the cascading sound of the waterfall beckoned her to join Jack. Her decision made, she half dove and half jumped into the pool, sending a huge spray of water onto Jack. The initial shock of the cool water quickly erased any thoughts of heat, dust, and stale air. A contented sigh escaped Sarah's mouth, and all tension escaped with it.

Sarah heard a noise in the water, and a thought quickly took her breath away. "There aren't any alligators here are there?"

"Definitely not," replied Jack. He waited a few seconds before adding, "Crocodiles perhaps, but no alligators."

"What?" Sarah shrieked as she fought against the water trying to make her way out.

"Calm down," urged Jack. "I was just kidding. Alligators are in the Americas. Crocodiles are in Africa." Sarah was still unsettled, and Jack added, "but there aren't any here."

"But I heard a noise in the water!"

"That was just me. Relax. There aren't any crocodiles here."

"Well, I hope they know they aren't supposed to be here."

Jack's laugh was reassuring, and Sarah let the water envelop her body and wash away any remaining tension. The sun on her face and the soothing sound of the water lulled Sarah into a state of serene blissfulness that pushed all thoughts from her mind. Eventually, awareness eased back into Sarah's mind, pulling her out from her meditative state. She wondered how much time had elapsed, but she didn't really care. This was the first time since she had left the Denver international airport that she had allowed herself to fully relax and be in the moment.

Sarah looked over at Jack and noticed a sly smile on his face. She started to ask what was up, but he broke the silence first.

"As a cultural anthropologist, you study cultural practices, right?"

"That's part of what cultural anthropologists do? Jack still wore the sly smile, and Sarah was beginning to grow more curious as to where this line of questioning was leading.

"What's your take on this social phenomenon?" Suddenly, Jack took his hands and pushed against the water, splashing water on the parts of Sarah's body that weren't already submerged under water.

Sarah realized what he was talking about, and the reason for the sly smile, a little too late. She had just opened her mouth to ask him what he was talking about when the splash entered her mouth and drenched the rest of her head. "Oh no, you didn't!" Coughing from the water she swallowed, she slapped at the water sending splashes back toward Jack. Soon, both were engaged in a water splashing war. "Ok. Ok. I give," shivered Sarah, as her body was no longer acclimated to the water.

"Are you cold? Let's get out and dry off." Jack helped Sarah out of the water, back onto the sandy beach, and across the rocks while Sarah's shivers grew in intensity. Once they were out, Jack hurried and grabbed a towel and sponged the water gently from Sarah's body. He then grabbed an even larger towel and wrapped it around her. Gradually, her shivers subsided. Between the sun and the breeze, Jack was air dried quickly. "I'm sorry. I didn't mean to make you cold."

"No. Don't apologize. It was fun. It's too bad I got cold because I was on the verge of winning our water splashing contest." Jack smiled, and Sarah felt the tingling return for the third time that day. Jack walked over to the acacia tree, and Sarah could feel the heat in her cheeks from blushing.

Jack untied his backpack and returned. "You haven't eaten anything since breakfast. I thought you might be hungry; so, I packed a light snack to hold you over until dinner tonight." Jack spread out a blanket on the ground and got a couple containers from his backpack, which he placed on top of the blanket.

Sarah opened the containers, finding cheese in one and fruit in another. Sarah picked some of the cheese and began to eat. "A glass of wine would go good with this."

Jack smiled slyly again and pulled out a bottle of wine wrapped in a cloth from his backpack. "Ask, and ye shall receive." He set the bottle of wine on the blanket and rummaged in his backpack producing two glasses. He opened the bottle of wine, and the removal of the cork made a popping sound. He poured each of them some wine and handed Sarah her glass.

Sarah smelled the wine, and an aroma of various fruits and grapefruit greeted her nose and rushed to her head.

"This is a Sauvignon Blanc that's produced here in Kenya," stated Jack.

"This is nice, no plastic cups."

"We're all about conservation," smiled Jack.

Sarah took a sip of the wine. Her shoulders relaxed as she sighed. "This is good wine."

"Living in Colorado, I'm sure you have your fair share of California wines. I hope this compares well with what you like."

"Oh, it's very good." Sarah ate another piece of cheese and drank some more wine. Soon she had finished a glass, and Jack poured some more for her. With the heat returning, Sarah shed the towel wrapped around her. Whether it was the sun, her relaxed state of mind, or the fact that she had not eaten much in a while, save for the cheese, Sarah soon felt the effects of the alcohol, which relaxed her even further. Alcohol sometimes made her chatty, and she could feel herself heading in that direction. "Was it my imagination, or do

Jill and Gacoki seem to like each other?"

"It's not your imagination. They do like each other, but both are afraid to let the other know. I think they make a good couple. They've known each other long enough. I would have thought one of them would have made a move by now."

Sarah and Jack both reached for the same piece of fruit, and their hands touched. Perhaps with the aid of the alcohol, the tingle Sarah had experienced earlier returned in full force. Her eyes inadvertently met his, and Jack's eyes drew her eyes to his like a magnet. Their eyes locked onto each other's, and Sarah could feel the palpable connection through their hands. The depth of his gaze captivated her, and she could not break her eyes away. His gaze issued a silent invitation that battered against the barriers within her. Something in the far reaches of her mind told her to break away, and she could see in his eyes that something was telling him likewise. Suddenly, they severed the connection and awkwardly stumbled for something to say.

Jack was the first to find words. "We probably better head back."

"Thank you for this. I had a great time."

"So did I."

As they headed back from their trip to the waterfall, Sarah searched for casual conversation to break the awkwardness that still hung over them like a cloud of guilt. "Have you always lived in Africa?"

"Mostly," Jack answered impassively. "When our parents and

grandfather were killed in the jeep accident, we were thirteen and went to Australia for five years. We had a cousin; her name was Catherine Wells. Although she was English, her late husband was Australian. We arrived in England one day, and she sent us to boarding school in Australia the next day."

"What?" Sarah asked incredulously. "You're kidding right?"

"I wish I were."

Sarah was beginning to understand the reason Jack knew little of his past as well as his lack of enthusiasm to know more. With a next of kin acting so apathetically after such personal loss, no wonder Jack didn't want to have anything to do with his past. Sarah could also better understand the relationship between Jack and Jill. They probably had to look after each other because no one else would. Maybe this was the reason Jill was not admitting her feelings toward Gacoki. Yet, Jill didn't seem to feel exactly the same way as Jack. Did Jill still feel it was her duty to protect Jack, or had Jack suffered another heartbreak beyond this one that she didn't know about. "What about breaks and summers? Didn't you stay with your cousin then?"

"On short breaks, we stayed at the school. For longer breaks and during the summer break, which was in December and January, we stayed with our cousin's late husband's family. One of the family friends was a park ranger, and Jill and I helped him whenever we could. Helping him reminded us of home here in Africa. Once we were eighteen, we left and came back here."

Jack seemed stoic in his description of the events, as if he were recalling a bad dream that someone had told him. No matter how impassive he seemed on the outside, he had to have hurt built up on the inside. Sarah wanted to hold Jack and tell him that everything would be alright, but the thought of the recent intimate moment they shared stopped her from doing so; she didn't want to give Jack the wrong idea. The thought of their touch and gaze invaded Sarah's mind, and she tried to dismiss it. She came up with a couple of reasons for the behavior. It was the alcohol. They were just caught up in the moment. She barely knew Jack, and he had been insensitive to her when they first met. She couldn't have real feelings for him. Wesley was her boyfriend. Maybe they didn't have the best of relationships, but he was always there for her. The realization that Wesley wasn't with her made her reframe her previous thought. Wesley was often with her. Sure, he may be somewhat self-absorbed but so could she. Sarah realized that she and Jack were walking in silence again. Even if she had a moment of weakness, she still wanted to show she cared for him as a friend. Were they friends? Even if they weren't, Jack had certainly helped her, which he didn't have to do. "What happened to the camp while you were gone?" she blurted. Maybe that wasn't the best question to ask, but she felt as though she needed to say something.

Jack was silent for a moment, perhaps dwelling on his own thoughts. He let out a barely audible sigh and answered. "Fortunately, our parents had everything planned in case something ever happened to them. Someone managed the place and paid the taxes and bills until we returned. That was the start of our financial woes."

"How so?" Sarah knew she could be prying into something that was none of her business, but Jack's answer didn't seem to add up. If someone attended to the place, how did that lead to any current financial problems? Apparently, Jack didn't see it as prying; he answered as impassively as he had answered her other questions.

"The person managing the camp really let it go and didn't have guests here. We had to rebuild our clientele and learn how to run a business. Everything in the camp was so old and rundown that we eventually had to replace it all. We ran out of our parents' money and had to get a loan from the bank."

"I'm so sorry. No wonder the boxes I'm looking through are in such a mess."

"Yeah." Jack gave a half-hearted chuckle that seemed out of place. "We just transferred everything over to the new building. Jill has been on to me to try some different things."

Sarah was silent as her mind retraced the conversation she had interrupted between Jill and Gacoki earlier that day.

"You don't have to pretend you don't know what I'm talking about. I heard the conversation that Jill, Gacoki, and you were having when I walked up to take us on our outing."

Sarah felt trapped in the middle of a squabble between siblings. "You mean when you slithered up?" She tried to divert Jack's attention from the matter but realized she really needed to face it head on. "I didn't really hear anything specific."

"I'm sorry. I'm not trying to put you in the middle of it. Contrary to what Jill may believe, I'm not against her ideas at all, but I believe that the main thing we need to do is expand our guest capacity. The tent you have is due to a cancellation. Even one cancellation hurts the business. And before you say anything, I'm not asking you to pay. Letting you stay is a gift I'm ... Jill and I are giving to you. I'm just trying to make the point that we need more guests."

"And you can't expand guest capacity without more capital."

"Precisely. Another problem we struggle against is perception."

"How so?"

"My great grandfather's era was associated with colonialism, which almost always led to changing the natural social systems of the colony along with the taking of natural resources. Some people still see us as a byproduct of colonialism."

"You seem to know quite a bit about cultural anthropology yourself," Sarah joked.

They continued walking in silence for several minutes until the outline of the camp gradually came into view. Sarah had conflicting emotions. The trip to the waterfall had been so exciting, and Jack had seemed so at ease. Everything after the unexpected and brief moment they shared had left her feeling apprehensive. Jack's revelations left her feeling sad for him. On top of that, she felt as though she had betrayed Wesley. She felt her emotions were having a civil war within her. The camp seemed a welcome respite for her embattled state.

Chapter 7

Sarah sighed as she saw the number of boxes left to go through. A new day, the same daunting task. Indecision gripped her at the thought of where to start. Jack had helped her the day before. Something about having someone help always seemed to make chores more bearable. Even though she knew this was a part of field research, and an exciting revelation was always only one document away, sometimes it still felt like drudgery. Sarah's indecision was interrupted by a noise and loud thuds on the staircase. She felt relieved when she saw Jack, Jill, and Gacoki come into the cluttered, gloomy basement.

"I brought reinforcements. Thought you might could use the help." Jack seemed more chipper this morning than when he had arrived back at the camp yesterday.

"Definitely. Thank you guys for helping me with this. I know there are other things you could be doing."

"No problem," replied Jill. "We pride ourselves in helping all of our guests, but you're also helping us find out more about our past."

Sarah wondered if that were a good thing considering what Jack had told her about being sent to boarding school in Australia after the death of their parents. They had all been kind to her, and she didn't want to pay that kindness back with more distressing revelations about their family.

Jill interrupted her thoughts. "Tell us what you need us to do."

"The materials from the Kenyan museum may not be labeled. I'm looking for any photos of Gordon Powell or any letters that may have his name on them. If you aren't sure about something, let me know, and I'll come look." Sarah organized the group, asking each person to start at a specific section in the basement. She explained that if a box didn't have anything relevant, then it could be put to the side. She also added that the boxes that had been searched could be put with the other boxes. Jack and Jill would know if they needed to keep anything, and those boxes could be put in a separate location. Unfortunately, Jack and Jill would still need to go through the boxes that Sarah and Gacoki had searched through, but the number of boxes would at least be less numerous.

As was the case yesterday, the stirred-up dust caused lots of sneezes. The stale air was thick with the scent of old paper, and Sarah's mind went back to the refreshing waterfall where the layers of dust were cleansed as if by ablution. Minute by minute, the group kept up the tedious task until three hours had passed. Sarah's hands felt chapped and as rough as sandpaper after the arduous task of handling each piece of paper in each box. Her breathing was in sync with the rustle of each document she turned. The ink had faded on so many documents that Sarah wondered that even if they did find something whether it would be intact and legible.

Suddenly, Jill let out a shriek. "Hey! I think I may have found something!"

Sarah's heart skipped a beat at the pronouncement. Both anticipation and trepidation jockeyed for position over her emotions. Anticipation finally won out. "Ooh. Let me see!" Sarah raced as quickly as she could through the obstacle course of boxes between her and Jill. Sarah felt as though she were in a dream as she made her way to Jill, one of those dreams where one tries to get somewhere only to be sidetracked by some challenge. When she finally reached Jill, she was breathing hard, sucking in the dusty air.

"It looks like a diary," chirped Jill.

Sarah held out trembling hands, and Jill carefully placed the leather-bound diary into Sarah's hands. The leather was worn but had hopefully preserved the contents much better than the boxes holding loose papers. Sarah had to purposely take a several deep breaths of dusty air as she purposefully willed her shaking hands to calm themselves. Slowly, she opened the cover. Although the pages were slightly worn, they were in good condition, and the ink was still well-preserved. She scanned the first page and was overcome by a rush of emotions, a mixture of relief, exuberance, and triumph. The treasure she had been seeking, the treasure that had launched her voyage to Kenya and this camp, had been discovered. She clutched the diary to her chest as if it were a security blanket. Her elation was momentarily interrupted by Jack.

"Well, what does it say?" inquired Jack.

Sarah opened the diary to the first page and began to read.

Chapter 8

Gordon checked his watch once more. "They're overdue."

"They'll get here when they get here," advised Kagiso.

"We'll be the ones setting up the camp. I just don't want to have to do it in the dark."

"Don't they have people who can help?

"Not ones who can help us setup."

"Well, it's a good thing that I thought to employ several people to help us. Besides, the tents are already set up. That's the main thing."

"I still don't want to have to do it in the dark."

"You've been through much worse, old friend. Besides, I think I hear them coming now."

"You have the hearing of an elephant," goaded Gordon.

"As long as I don't have as large ears as one."

Gordon could now make out the outline of several approaching vehicles.

"It looks like they're bringing the entire castle," chuckled Kagiso.

"Everything but the moat. However, I don't think any of them live in a castle. Now you see what I meant by getting everything set up."

As the first jeep came to a stop, Viscount Anthony Montagu immediately stood up and shouted at the top of his lungs, "Gordon! Kagiso! It's so good to see both of you." He immediately jumped from the jeep and ran to Gordon and Kagiso, giving each a tremendous bear hug. Anthony pried himself between Gordon and Kagiso and draped an arm over each one's shoulders. "I can't believe it's been six years since last we saw each other."

A second jeep pulled up behind the first one, and then four trucks after that. Three females stepped out of the second jeep and stretched their legs from the long, hot journey. As the three looked around, Gordon could tell that by the looks on their faces that the realization had just set in. They definitely weren't in London, or even Nairobi. Nairobi, with some of its grand hotels, served many Englishmen or Englishwomen who visited Africa. Between teatime and croquet on the lawn, the heat and scenery were the only reminders that they were no longer in England. But here in the savanna the story was much different. Although they would still have teatime, that was about the only reminder of home they would have. The truckful of items they had brought with them might suggest otherwise, but those items were mere token items meant to preserve their feelings of social status, security blankets of a sort. One roar of a lion overcoming the sound of a record being played on a gramophone and the security blanket was gone. Gordon was certainly not questioning the bravery of the English. In fact, during the war, the English were some of the bravest men he had seen. Perhaps it was the empire that the English had built that accustomed them to an unbreakable spirit and to following a sense of order and tradition even in the face of overwhelming odds. His problem was with the English who thought they were better than everyone else. The sense of arrogance and entitlement could get a person killed out here quicker than anything else. Gordon realized what he was thinking and backed off. If he were honest, a particular nationality wasn't typically more prone than any other to underestimate the danger in the wilds. Tourists, no matter their nationality, who acted self-important and careless were the danger. In fact, two of them were now getting out of the first jeep and walking toward Gordon, Kagiso, and Anthony.

The blonde Englishwoman was leading the way. She had to be an aristocrat since she was in the jeep with Anthony, but she somehow seemed a contradiction of features. She possessed a captivating and bold presence and carried herself with grace, but she didn't seem entitled. Her unruly golden hair framed a face that exuded mischief, but also warmth. The man behind her however, was an easy read. He was an extremely stuffy and pompous looking gentleman who exuded an air of self-importance and haughty disdain that he wore like a scented cologne. He was meticulously and opulently dressed. His angular face and sharp features combined with a high forehead and slicked-back black hair to form an image of icy aloofness and disdain. He had yet to look anyone directly in the eyes.

His look and mannerisms were not an act; it was a part of him, bred into him by a long-standing lineage, shackled to him by an aristocratic upbringing.

"Let me introduce my sister, Lady Amelia Montagu," announced Anthony.

Gordon wasn't sure whether he was to bow or to lightly take her hand, but the thoughts quickly faded. He was who he was, and he wasn't about to start acting differently now. "Lady Amelia. It's a pleasure to meet you." That was all the niceties he would give. Yet, it didn't faze her.

A beautiful smile that caused her green eyes to sparkle like emeralds in the sun preceded an intoxicating laugh. "Oh, please. It's Amelia. *Lady* is just too stuffy and formal for friends of my brother." Amelia's voice wasn't what Gordon was expecting. She had a proper English accent like her brother. Her voice itself was hard to describe. It lowered in pitch when she wanted to emphasize something. It seemed a mixture of velvet, smokiness, and a hint of rawness while still being smooth. It was quite alluring and sensual.

"I must insist that you are called by your proper title." The man had enunciated each word in a proper English accent that dripped with pretentiousness. He spoke as though Amelia were one of his possessions rather than an independent person.

"And this is Marquess of Brackley, Thomas Mowbray ... and Amelia's fiancé," added Anthony. "His father is the Duke of Bridgewater."

Gordon was shocked, but he didn't show it. Although he knew

little of the two people he had just met, his first impressions told him a lot. He had never seen two more mismatched people. This obviously had to be an arranged engagement. He wasn't going to give whatever the man was called the satisfaction of a greeting.

"You know," goaded Amelia. "I didn't learn until right before we booked passage that you and Kagiso saved my brother's life during the Great War."

"Men don't talk about those things to women, Lady Amelia," interjected Thomas in a manner Gordon thought was admonishment.

"How would you know?" provoked Amelia. "You weren't in the Great War. I'm not sure how you escaped it."

Gordon stifled a chuckle. Thomas had his work cut out for him if he was going to try to subjugate Amelia. Gordon could tell that the provocation rattled Thomas somewhat.

"I've told you before. I had an injury that prevented the Expeditionary Forces from taking me. Besides, the son of a duke shouldn't have to go off to war anyway."

"But the son of an earl can?"

"An earl and a duke are not the same."

"Yes. As you've told me often."

Gordon wanted to call Thomas a smug son of a bitch, but he wanted the bickering to end so that the camp could be set up. "Kagiso and I are glad to be your guides."

"I wondered what an American was doing living in Africa," stated Amelia. "I hear you are from the wild west in the United States."

"One could also wonder why anyone would want to go on a safari as a prelude to getting married. This isn't an afternoon tea. Africa is a dangerous place for someone who is used to the finer things of life. I must wonder if you take the dangers of a safari seriously."

"Listen here now," retorted Thomas. "I'll not have a ruffian talk that way to my fiancée."

"I'm not a babysitter, Tom." Gordon knew that calling him Tom would definitely rile him, but he didn't care.

"You will refer to me by my proper title, sir." Thomas apparently knew that wouldn't happen, and he walked away sulking while Amelia merely laughed.

The three women in the second jeep, Amelia's friends, could wait no longer and they giddily approached Gordon.

Not waiting for an introduction, one of them began talking to Gordon. "I'm Lady Mary Alexander. I was so excited when I learned that our guide was the famous American hunter, Gordon Powell. You were the one who killed the man-eater of Mara and the man-eaters of Noonchuta. Tell us about them."

Gordon nodded to Kagiso. "It's as much of an accomplishment of Kagiso, who is an expert when it comes to Kenyan wildlife, as it was for me. Kagiso can tell you about them."

Kagiso emitted a single, hearty laugh. "Don't let Gordon fool you. He did what many others could not do. The man-eater of Mara was a lion. That lion had killed dozens of people. Gordon killed him with a single shot. It was during the day. Once a lion gets used to humans, it loses its fear of them and hunts during the day, which is when humans are active. The man-eaters of Noonchuta were a pair of leopards. Leopards never really lose their fear of humans; so, they attack at night."

"Why do lions and leopards eat humans?" quizzed Mary.

Apparently over his sulking, Thomas had rejoined the group. "Really. Must we discuss such things?"

"I want to hear the answer," insisted Amelia.

Gordon wondered if she did indeed want to know or if she was merely trying to provoke Thomas further. Perhaps both. Amelia did seem a curious type.

Thomas huffed and went into his tent, which already had his belongings inside. Kagiso's men, under the close guidance of Thomas' valet or butler, had made quick work of the unloading. Of course, Thomas' tent was the first to be ready.

Kagiso continued with the explanation. "Humans are not the natural diet of these cats. Most of the time, the animal is injured. In the case of leopards, they may become man-eaters because overkilling of animals may have deprived them of their food source. In some cases, the cats are old. Humans are easy to catch."

"That's why societies are established that are led by the nobility," called Thomas, still in his tent.

"I imagine there is some truth to that," admitted Gordon. "A human can't outrun most dangerous animals."

"The most dangerous animals are humans themselves," added Amelia.

"Again, that's why the need for societies exists," echoed Thomas.

Kagiso continued despite the interruption. "Even then, these animals don't usually start out killing humans. They may taste the blood of someone who died, and then they start going after people."

Anthony must have read the trepidation on the faces of Amelia's friends. "Don't worry. We have guides. Just do as they say, and we should all have a great time."

"I hope everyone brought practical clothing," informed Gordon. On many of the safaris I've led, people want to wear pith helmets, carry a sidearm, and wear binoculars around their necks. They look like fools."

As if on cue, the tent flap on Thomas' tent slapped the canvas siding of the tent, and Thomas exited dressed just as Gordon had described. Apparently, Thomas' eavesdropping had not caught the last statement Gordon had made. "Do I look the part?" Gordon shook his head, and Amelia laughed. "What's so funny?" Thomas face grew red. "I never have understood American humor."

"It's just like British humor, just not as biting," answered Gordon.

"Good show. Good show indeed, sir." Amelia emphasized the second sentence in a voice like a smooth, aged whisky that perfectly complemented the sparkle in her evergreen eyes, which momentarily disarmed Gordon.

🐘 🐘 🐘

In her tent, Amelia began tidying up the objects that had been haphazardly placed in various places by a group of men who had no clue where they went. This safari was to be her last hurrah as a single woman. It seemed more like a ticking clock speeding its way toward married life with the Marquess of Brackley, Thomas Mowbray, who would become the Duke of Bridgewater when his father died. The tent closed in on her, the perfect metaphor she thought for her current state. She felt like the condemned who were asked if they had a final request before they met the executioner. This safari was her final request, not that she requested it. Going on safari in east Africa was the fashionable thing to do nowadays. Her brother, Anthony, was the one who suggested she go in order to help get her mind off the upcoming wedding. That would have been much easier if Thomas had not come along.

Her parents didn't know quite what to do with her; they never did. She was a square peg they tried to fit into a round hole. She had always been independent, mischievous according to many. She couldn't really blame her parents. After all, she was of age to be married, and her parents had arranged a marriage to the only son of a duke. And Thomas wasn't a bad man. He fit his role perfectly. Her situation was the envy of most young women in England. Most would love to be the wife of a high-ranking nobleman and throw high society parties. After the Great War and the Spanish Flu, she wondered if such things would even exist anymore. They were probably the casualties of a bygone era.

Her mind turned to the news she learned on the trip to Nairobi. She knew her brother had been injured in the war, but he had never spoken of how his life was saved by Gordon and Kagiso or of their recuperation in a base hospital. On the trip, Anthony had told her about the stories Kagiso told to pass the time. She thought this trip was as much for him as for her. Other times, they would play cards or play pranks on the nurses. The war had to have bothered Anthony, but he never let it show, in public anyway. According to Anthony, the Great War had really taken its toll on Gordon. Gordon had been hell-bent on a suicide mission after learning about the death of his under-aged brother. Rather than death, his mission brought him hero status. He still sought death, she thought, though the circumstances in Africa weren't as amenable to death as they were in war-torn France. Perhaps the reason he hunted man-eaters was for the possibility of death. She had heard nothing about him hunting for sport. The only hunting she had heard about was man-eating lions and leopards. Just as the Germans were his enemy in the war, the man-eaters played that role in Kenya.

And speaking of Gordon, there was something about him that intrigued her. It could have partially been his looks. He was as rugged as the pictures she had seen of the Rocky Mountains, hard and weather-beaten, but majestic. From what she could tell of the hair that protruded from his hat, it was a dark, chestnut brown. He had a thick mustache, no beard but certainly dark stubble. Everything about him was deliberate, from his movements to his honest speech.

All-in-all, he was a good-looking man with a hard, square jaw that readily contrasted with Thomas' sharp, angular features. There was something besides his looks though that intrigued her. He exuded a confidence that came not from a title or noble birth but from living a hard, rugged life. Perhaps his self-reliance was another feature that captivated her. She was used to living in a world where nobility relied on valets, butlers, and you name it. As she thought more about Gordon Powell, she realized that he was perhaps the only man who didn't give in to her charms. Usually, she would have a man eating from her hand within a matter of minutes. She knew she was pretty, not as pretty as some, but her personality was what truly captivated the men she had known. Yet, Gordon was not swayed by her. Of course, neither was Thomas, but she didn't count him. He was too self-absorbed to notice anyone other than himself.

Yet for all of Gordon's outward-appearing confidence, he was a bruised man. She didn't need Anthony to tell her that. She could see into the depths of Gordon's eyes, into his soul to see the tortured man he was. He was an enigma, strong on the outside but a man definitely in need of healing on the inside. Perhaps this safari would be interesting after all.

Chapter 9

Sarah carefully closed the leather cover to the diary. There was more there to be read, but Sarah felt spent. Although she wanted to read further, she also wanted to fully absorb what she had read so far and piece it together with the other information she knew. In her line of work, one couldn't go too fast, else something would be overlooked. For a moment, she had forgotten that she was with others. Then, Jill's voice brought her back to the present, and she was once again aware of the stale air and dim light of the basement.

"Wow! That is an interesting story. I have never heard any of that." Jill paused a moment, and a sly look appeared in her eyes. "Well, now we know where Jack gets his personality from."

"Very funny, sis."

"Your great grandfather saved lives. Surely, that must change your impression of him a little," implored Sarah.

"It does." Jack let a slight sigh escape, and he straightened his shoulders. "At least now I know that he didn't hunt for sport."

"We've seen a picture of Gordon. Is there a picture of Amelia in the box?" inquired Jill.

Sarah looked through the pictures in the box and pulled out two of them. "I suppose this is her." The first picture was of a group of four people. "One of the people in this photo is Gordon. The other three must be Amelia, Anthony, and Thomas." She showed the picture to Jack and Jill. "The other photo here is just of a woman standing beside of a tent, but it's the same woman who was in the first photo."

Jill held a photo in each hand. "Even though these are old and aren't in color, Amelia exudes the free-spiritedness described in her diary. She's very pretty. Well, we've found the materials you were looking for." Jill looked at Sarah, and Sarah sensed that Jill could tell she was spent. "They aren't going anywhere. Sarah, why don't you take tomorrow off and let Jack take you on a personal safari?"

"I need to take a group out tomorrow." Jack had the same impassive tone he had on the trip back from the waterfall.

Sarah wondered if he was upset with her for some reason or if the unexpected, shared moment between the two of them had bothered Jack as much as it had bothered her.

"Gacoki can do that, can't you?" Jack's tone had evidently not dampened Jill's determination.

"Of course, I'd be glad to," replied Gacoki.

"It's settled then." Jill put her hands on her hips in a display that added authority to her declaration.

Jack, obviously beaten, conceded. "We leave early in the morning."

The next morning, Sarah waited in the dining tent for Jack. She was seated at a table. A few of the other guests were eating a hearty breakfast in preparation for whatever adventures they were having. Sarah yawned just as Jack walked up.

"Did you not sleep well last night?"

"Not very." Sarah covered her mouth as another yawn escaped her mouth. "I was so excited about finding the information that I kept wondering what else was in the diary."

"As my sister said, it's not going anywhere. Hopefully, you'll see today why people find safaris so interesting. And maybe you'll see some of the same scenery and animals that Lady Amelia saw about one hundred years ago."

"Those animals must be pretty old by now." Sarah meant that as a joke, but as sleepy as she was, she didn't know whether it came across that way.

"Well, the same types of animals," clarified Jack.

"I meant that as a joke."

"I think you might better work on your presentation." Jack smiled for the first time in two days, and the adrenaline caused by his smile began to work magic and rejuvenate her.

"Hopefully, I won't fall asleep before I see all of this."

"You know. Kenya is famous for its coffee. Have you tried any yet? It may be just the thing to keep you energized today."

"No. I haven't actually. I usually grab Starbucks at home."

"That's the equivalent of a coffee cocktail. What you'll find in camp is some of the freshest and best coffee you've ever tasted. I'll get you a cup."

Jack departed to get coffee, and Sarah took the chance to yawn while he was away. Soon, Jack returned with a steaming cup of coffee. "I didn't know if you preferred a cup or mug. Since we predominantly have cups, and I didn't want to scrounge around for a mug, you have a cup."

"A cup is fine." Sarah could smell the aromatic scent of the coffee before Jack had even set it in front of her. She could detect notes of citrus in the rich and bold fragrance, and the fragrance invited her to take a sip. Although this was definitely not a macchiato or a latte, the coffee offered a complex flavor. Although she was by no means a coffee connoisseur and couldn't detect the subtleties of flavors, it was one of the best cups of coffee she had had. Each sip reinvigorated her. She felt more awake after the cup, but still couldn't suppress another yawn.

"Maybe we'd better make that two cups!" Jack exclaimed as he went to refill her cup.

The second cup of coffee definitely did the trick, and Sarah was wide awake and refreshed. Jack led her to the jeep and helped her climb in. Soon, they were off on their sightseeing adventure. The early morning sun gave a warm, golden-hued glow to the African landscape. The jeep rumbled across the savanna, shaking Sarah from side to side, and her senses came alive. She could smell the scent of earth and grass and hear the calls of birds over the rumbling jeep. The vast landscape extended, seemingly endless in all directions with golden grasses undulating from the breeze and small bushes dotting the landscape as far as the eye could see. Sarah noticed the numerous acacia trees with their flat tops and thorny branches. Over the sound of the engine, Jack pointed out a baobab tree. It was a massive tree with a swollen trunk.

"Baobab trees help keep the soil humid, and they slow erosion due to their massive root systems," explained Jack. "When you hear the phrase *tree of life* in Africa, people are talking about the baobab tree because it provides water and shelter for many types of animals."

"They look strange, upside down even. It looks as if a giant plucked up the tree by the roots and slammed the top of the tree into the ground leaving the roots where the top of the tree should be."

"I never thought of it that way," commented Jack, "but you're right. I'll have to remember that for future safaris. Sometimes it just takes someone else to bring a fresh perspective to what one is used to seeing on a daily basis."

As Sarah scanned the savanna, the first wildlife she saw were towering giraffes as they leisurely ate the leaves and twigs from acacia trees, chewing aslant. Sarah laughed.

"What's funny?" inquired Jack.

"I was just laughing at how the giraffes chew their food. Their jaws seem to go at an angle rather than straight up and down."

"Acacia trees can have long thorns among the leaves, but giraffes can use their tongues to maneuver around the thorns and only gather leaves. They chew their cud the way cows do, but they also chew that way to keep thorns from piercing their lips in case they were chewing long thorns. You've never seen a giraffe with a pierced lip, have you?"

Sarah rolled her eyes. "Ouch. That sounds painful just thinking about it." Sarah continued laughing.

"What are you laughing about now?"

"Your attempt at safari humor about giraffes with pierced lips. Have you ever been to Disney World?"

"No. Are you comparing this safari to Disney World?"

"No. There is an attraction called the *Jungle Cruise*. As you're waiting to ride, you pass through this 1920s setup with old décor. You get on a boat with lots of other people, and the captain of the boat makes corny jokes throughout the ride."

"So, you're saying that our camp has old décor, and I'm like the corny boat captain?"

"That's not what I meant. I like the setup of your camp. What you said just reminded me of the jokes they make on the ride."

"Well, apparently, if I ever stop doing this, it sounds like I could have a job at Disney World, and I wouldn't even have to learn the jokes."

"Yeah. Something like that." Sarah flashed a smile.

"Well, keep your eyes peeled, as we leave this *giraffic jam*, and I'll try not to disappoint with the jokes."

Sarah's eyes danced over the landscape looking for the next sight. Jack pointed, and Sarah followed the direction of his finger to a pride of lions resting peacefully in the shade of the umbrella canopies of acacia trees. The lions had a majestic look that conveyed their status as king of the beasts. As the jeep approached a watering hole, Sarah saw several elephants, some drinking water while others played in the water like a group of kids. Two elephants appeared to wrestle in the water, and she saw one spray water from its trunk to either cool itself or cleanse off the dust from its thick hide. One elephant heralded their approach with a trumpet blast.

"Ok. What's large and gray and cites poetry?"

"I think I'm going to regret this, but let's hear it." Sarah scrunched up her nose.

"T. S. Elephant."

"I think that's the worst dad joke I've ever heard. Maybe you should build these jokes into the safari. It would be your version of Disney World's Jungle Cruise."

"I'll stop with the jokes and tell you some important facts about elephants. Do you know why elephants have such big ears?"

"Are you sure this isn't going to be another bad joke?"

"No this is serious. African elephants have larger ears than Asian elephants. Actually, some say that their ears are shaped like the continent of Africa. They can use their ears to fan their bodies to help cool themselves. Their ears also have lots of blood vessels close to the surface. The blood vessels help elephants store heat, which they can release at night. They also use their trunks to cover their backs with mud to help cool them off. The mud also acts as a bug repellent."

"Is that elephant scratching itself?" Sarah pointed to an elephant rubbing against something.

"It is."

"What is that thing? It looks like a fossilized tree that was broken off."

"It's a termite mound. Elephants will sometimes rub against a termite mound to relieve an itch."

"Does the mound not collapse?"

"No. They are incredibly strong as you can see to support the weight of the elephant."

At another watering hole, Sarah saw the tops of submerged hippos. She shivered upon seeing crocodiles with their fake smiles. Jack explained that crocodiles do not have facial muscles that allow them to smile. It was merely a visual perception. Sarah continued to see a variety of animals, herds of zebras and wildebeests moving across the savanna, impalas and gazelles, wildebeests, and several rhinos. On the trip back, Jack pointed out a leopard atop a tree.

As the jeep made its way back to camp, Sarah suddenly pointed to a pack of animals. "Are those hyenas?"

Jack looked to where Sarah was pointing. "Those are African painted dogs. Some people consider them the best hunters in the savanna."

"Why is that?"

"They can run at a sustained rate of up to thirty-five miles per hour for over three miles. The dogs will switch off as lead, and one or two dogs will stay about one hundred yards behind, in case the prey starts to circle back. They usually catch their prey when it collapses from exhaustion." Jack pointed as the jeep continued. "Now over there is the fastest mammal on land, the cheetah. Cheetahs can reach speeds of up to sixty, or even seventy, miles per hour in around three seconds, but they can only sustain this speed for a short period of time. African painted dogs are the marathon runners, and cheetahs are the sprinters."

"Are we getting close to camp?"

"We'll be there in a few minutes. Did the safari bore you?"

"On the contrary. This was one of the most exciting things I've done."

"I bet you've never seen such exotic wildlife before."

"Only in zoos."

"Don't get me started on zoos." A scowl suddenly appeared on Jack's face.

The jeep hit a bump that sent Sarah bouncing what felt like a foot into the air. Sarah clutched the jeep with her right hand to steady herself. She wondered if he had done so on purpose at her mention of zoos. Jack seemed to be driving faster, and she swayed back and forth in her seat like a person who had never been on a ship before. Occasionally, her right shoulder bumped into the door frame of the jeep, and Sarah wondered if she would have a large bruise or be sore afterwards. They were quiet for a few minutes, and all Sarah could hear was the whir of the jeep's engine and the grinding noise the tires made.

Jack broke the silence. "So, why didn't your boyfriend come along?"

"He's busy." Her answer came instinctively. "He always seems to be busy."

"Are you two going to get married?"

The question caught Sarah off guard, like one of the potholes the jeep would occasionally hit. She wasn't sure how to answer and must have taken more than the expected amount of time to answer that question.

"I'm sorry," apologized Jack. "I shouldn't have asked that. It's none of my business."

Jack's comment granted Sarah enough time to regain her composure. "No. That's fine. I think we're both comfortable with each other, but I'm not sure about marriage. What about you? Do you have a girlfriend?"

Sarah felt vindicated, as now Jack seemed to be caught off guard.

His mouth moved a couple of times before he finally found the wherewithal to answer. "Not in a while. I thought there was someone. We were engaged." He paused as if considering whether to say more or as if remembering a dream from the past. "She was a guest here a few years ago. I thought she liked this lifestyle, but I think she saw this as a vacation. Eventually, that feeling wore off with the daily activities and behind the scenes work of running a camp such as ours, and she left."

Sarah let out a huff, either from the jeep hitting another pothole or from her spirits dropping at the sound of hurt and betrayal in Jack's voice. "I'm sorry," was all she could manage to say. She wanted to say more, but what does one say to something such as that?

Sarah looked over at Jack. His eyes were straight ahead. She couldn't read his eyes directly, but she sensed he was driving in a daze, one of those times when you drive for miles before suddenly wondering how you got where you were.

"That's ok. I just haven't found anyone since then. I don't know that I will. My life is here. The women who come here stay for a week, maybe two at the most, and they're usually here with their boyfriends or husbands. My chances of finding someone are about as likely as you seeing that tiger or alligator you mentioned."

Sarah wondered if her being alone had prompted him to ask the question. Did he see her as a potential love interest since she was here by herself? That was probably not the case though because he knew she had a boyfriend. He was probably just curious as to why her boyfriend had chosen to remain in the States. Sarah could feel the melancholy surrounding Jack as if it were a visible windbreaker sheltering him from the beating wind. Various responses ran through her mind until she settled on one. "Well, it just takes one. You don't need a herd of women."

Jack laughed heartily, his body shaking more than just from the vibration of the jeep. "Handling one woman is a handful. I couldn't even begin to imagine dealing with a whole herd of women. I'll stick to showing tourists the herds of animals!"

The jeep rumbled to a stop at the camp, Jack was a gentleman and walked around the jeep to open the door for Sarah. Riding in the jeep for so long, Sarah teetered out of the jeep. She still could feel her body swaying to and fro as if she were on the deck of a ship in a rough swell. Her body coursed with a mixture of excitement and exhaustion. The day had been wonderful, but the Kenyan coffee had worn off. She coughed and swore at the dust that issued from her mouth. "I think I'm wearing half of Kenya after that safari."

"We don't usually have guests mimic the behavior of animals they've seen on the safari."

Sarah's eyebrows rose, and her head cocked slightly to the side. "What do you mean?"

"I thought maybe you were mimicking the elephants by putting dirt on you to keep yourself cool and to keep the bugs off." Jack's deadpan expression broke into a slight smile.

"And I thought the jokes would end after the safari."

"I don't charge extra for humor."

"That's a good thing."

"Another good thing is that I have the perfect remedy for you. Have a drink at the bar to wash the dust down and go to your tent in about fifteen minutes."

"The drink does sound good, but I don't know about swallowing dust, but I guess alcohol would do a good job cutting the dust while masking the taste." Jack marched off with a purpose, and Sarah made her way, still swaying, over to the bar. She hoped the bartender hadn't seen her swaying; he'd probably think she was already drunk. Would he care though? Probably not. Sarah asked the bartender to surprise her, and he returned within a few minutes with an elaborate looking drink. Sarah took a sip, closed her eyes, and savored the taste. It was truly delightful. "Does this drink have a name?"

"I call it a Monkey's Butt."

"A drink this good needs a better name."

"Good point. I'll work on that."

Sarah finished the drink and ordered another. After she'd finished the second drink, she figured it had been at least fifteen minutes. She walked to her tent, already feeling better. "Jack?"

"On the verandah," he answered.

Sarah wondered what was going on as she made her way through the tent to the verandah. Jack was standing next to a tub of soapy water. "What's this?"

"This is a traditional safari bath. You have a canvas tub, a bottle of wine and a gorgeous view. This will be the most relaxing bath you've ever had. Enjoy, and I'll see you at dinner." Jack left, and Sarah shed her dusty clothes and stepped into the canvas tub. The water slowly enveloped her tired body, and a contented smile spread across her face as she closed her eyes. The warm soapy water felt good against her skin, and the dust and grime dissolved along with her thoughts. Eventually, one thought entered her head, a recollection from an entry in Amelia's diary.

🐘 🐘 🐘

Gordon led the safari group back into camp in the afternoon. They had left at sunrise and had walked on foot for hours. The sun had been scorching, and the English party showed the sign of wear. Thomas was limping due to the blisters on his feet, and he immediately went into his tent once they arrived back at camp. Gordon looked at Amelia as she wiped the sweat from her face. "This is not like playing croquet on a manicured lawn with servants holding trays of cool drinks for you."

"You, sir, are not funny. At least I hope that was your attempt at a joke and not what you think I do all day."

"I'm not really sure what you do all day," Gordon replied.

"And I'm not sure what you do all day," quipped Amelia. "For all I know, you extract exorbitant amounts of money from your guests and put on a show once a month of how tough life is here while sitting in the shade the rest of the month."

Gordon chuckled. "Touche! That wouldn't be a bad life though."

"Which one, croquet or sitting here in the shade?"

"Either one."

"Croquet is boring after the first couple of times. I need more excitement. So, just between us, did you enjoy putting us through the gauntlet today?"

"I try to give everyone their money's worth for those exorbitant fees I charge. Just between us, Kagiso and I aren't taking any money from your brother. We're doing it as a favor. We all supported each other during our encounter in the war and in the hospital. We're all like brothers. What he's paying just covers costs; there is no profit for us. To answer your question though, I did enjoy seeing Thomas struggle, especially after I told him he was wearing the wrong clothing and shoes for our excursion today."

Amelia was quiet for a moment. She couldn't find the words she wanted to say. Finally, all she said was, "Thank you."

"I know just the thing to make you feel better. Wait here in the shade for a few minutes, and I'll come get you."

After a few minutes, Amelia had dozed off, and the next thing she knew, Gordon was shaking her gently. He held out his hand, and Amelia took it.

"Come with me."

Amelia followed him along a path until they came to another tent that she had not seen. Gordon opened the flap. Once she entered, he shut it. Amelia was unsure of his intentions and her heartbeat quickened. Then, she saw a bathtub at the end of the tent with a view of the landscape. The canvas tub was identical to the one she had in her private tent, and she was curious as to why Gordon brought her here. Once she approached the tub full of water, she understood. The view of the landscape was stunning.

"This is not as fancy as you're used to, and you have no lady's maid, unless a baboon or red-tailed monkey wants the job," teased Gordon. "I guarantee you that you'll enjoy the bath though."

"I know one side is open so that I can enjoy the view, but can anyone else on that side enjoy the view in here?"

"The only peeping Tom you'll get here may be a giraffe, but he'll be more interested in the leaves above you than in seeing you."

"I'm insulted, sir." Amelia couldn't help but smile as she said it. "Whenever I'm present, the attention is always on me."

"Well, if you see a giraffe and want it focused on you, I would suggest you wear leaves! For anyone else, I'll put this sign that says *occupied* across the front flap." Gordon exited the tent and closed the flap behind him.

Amelia stripped and immersed herself in the water. She let out a long sigh. "This is much better than croquet."

🐘 🐘 🐘

After Sarah's relaxing bath, she felt her energy return, and she was determined to look at Amelia's diary and discover more pieces of the puzzle. She quickly dressed and went to the dining tent to eat dinner. Afterwards, she asked Jack, Jill, and Gacoki if they wanted to accompany her to the basement in the staff lodge to read more of the diary. They eagerly agreed, and soon the four were in the basement gathered around Sarah as she held Amelia's diary. Sarah's hands shook slightly from the excitement she felt to peer into the past of Amelia's and Gordon's lives.

Jill broke the anticipation that permeated the room. "I'm so excited to hear what happens next."

Sarah looked up, smiled, and began to read.

Chapter 10

The campfire blazed in front of them and shot angry sparks as Kagiso threw more wood onto the fire and sat beside Gordon. Anthony passed around crystal wine glasses, and Thomas pulled the corks out of two bottles of 1900 Chateau Margaux Bordeaux. As serving wine was beneath Thomas, Anthony walked around the circle of people by the fire and poured some into each glass. Soon, Amelia, her three friends, Thomas, Anthony, Kagiso, and Gordon were all laughing and drinking wine. Thomas pulled the corks out of two more bottles, and Anthony refilled the glasses. Lady Mary begged Kagiso to tell some stories.

Kagiso thought for a moment and began. "I've seen Maasai warriors steal food from a pride of lions eating a wildebeest they had killed." His eyes sparkled, either from the story or the wine. "Three warriors had spears and walked confidently up to the lions while they were eating." Kagiso was temporarily interrupted by a gasp from Lady Mary. "At first, the lions stared at the approaching warriors. Then one lion retreated. Then, two retreated. Eventually, they all left and watched a short distance from their kill. One of the warriors cut off a haunch of the kill in a matter of seconds. They had to do this quickly, or the lions would regather their courage and attack. Once the warriors had gathered a portion, they would walk confidently back, allowing the lions to return to their kill."

"How ghastly," snorted Thomas. "Eating meat that had been taken in such a manner sounds barbaric."

Kagiso looked to Thomas, "An old Maasai proverb says that a zebra takes its stripes wherever it goes."

Amelia snorted wine through her nose at the comment and began coughing. She looked at Thomas, but he was searching for the next bottle of wine to uncork. She doubted that Thomas had even caught Kagiso's jab at him.

"You have such interesting stories, Kagiso. Please tell us another one," pleaded Lady Mary.

Just as Kagiso was about to tell a story, an antelope curiously wandered into the camp. Amelia's friends gasped and the blood drained from their faces. Kagiso motioned with his hand for everyone to remain calm. Kagiso held out his glass, and the antelope approached as if he had done this many times before. As everyone stared, the antelope drank some of the wine from the glass and then turned and walked out of the camp. "He is a friend of mine," beamed Kagiso. "Now, you will have your own story to tell."

Once the antelope had disappeared, Thomas stood, and in a clipped accent began to lecture Kagiso. "That was very expensive wine that you just wasted. It was kind of me to let you and Gordon drink with us in the first place, but I will not stand for this waste. No,

I shall not."

Gordon remained seated. Amelia could tell he was angry, but his voice was calm in contrast to Thomas' berating tone. "You have three choices: sit down now, I knock you down, or I throw you to that giant eland antelope and let it gore you."

Thomas huffed at the challenge, but sat down, mumbling to himself. He didn't say another word the rest of the night, but the outburst dampened the enthusiasm that had been shared among the group moments earlier. Everyone finished the wine they had, careful not to guzzle it or pour it out lest Thomas criticize anyone further. One by one, everyone turned in for the night.

The next day, around noon, Gordon had his arm around Kagiso's shoulders as Kagiso helped him into camp. Gordon's shirt was ripped from claw marks, and he was bleeding from marks on his chest and arms. Amelia and Thomas followed closely behind, and Thomas went immediately to his tent. Amelia remained with Gordon and Kagiso.

"What happened?" Anthony had been standing outside as the group came in, but he was frozen in place. Amelia thought the sight must have brought back memories from the Great War.

Gordon was in obvious pain. "Your sister and future brother-in-law decided to go walk around on their own. Lord Lion Liver over there," Gordon motioned with his head toward Thomas' tent, "shot a rifle into the air to scare off some lions. Then his gun jammed. Fortunately, I was nearby. I drew the attention of the lions, and one jumped on me. I literally had to wrestle the lion. The others were ready to close in. Kagiso heard the gunfire and came to help.

Fortunately, for me, that scared off the lions. I've never seen two people more careless out here." Gordon clenched his teeth before he could continue. He looked directly at Amelia. "What were you thinking? I should have let the lions have the both of you."

"I know a little first aid." Amelia was calm, and her voice was steady, but her eyes held back tears. "I'll clean and wrap the wounds."

Kagiso led Gordon to his tent, followed by Amelia.

As soon as Gordon was in his tent, Thomas came out in a huff. "Who does he think he is to talk that way to someone above his social status? He is getting paid quite handsomely to take care of us."

The hair stood up on Anthony's arms and he looked directly into Thomas' eyes. "You'd better be glad that nothing happened to Amelia. If something had, I would have shot you myself." Anthony turned and walked away.

Late that night, Amelia couldn't sleep. After tossing and turning for what seemed like hours, she got up and put a robe over her nightgown. She exited her tent and walked to the campfire. Bright orange coals glowed and shimmered. Amelia stirred the coals with a poker and coaxed a small flame from them. She used some kindling to get the flames higher and then carefully placed several pieces of wood on the fire. Soon, the fire was burning, illuminating the area around the pit. Amelia sat on a log near the fire and could feel the warmth from the fire stretch out to meet her. She didn't have to wonder what kept her from sleeping. Her mind juggled a myriad of thoughts back and forth. She felt like a pariah. She had friends, but she didn't fit in with the life that was expected of her. She couldn't imagine marrying Thomas, and she dreaded the life they would have together. Her family was counting on her marriage to Thomas. It would raise their social status even higher. Ending the relationship now would be an unrecoverable blow to her family. They would be social pariahs. On top of that, she was developing feelings for Gordon. Her family would never understand that. She wondered if she was attracted to Gordon simply because she didn't want Thomas. Perhaps it was a passing infatuation. But she didn't feel that to be the case. Something in her very core knew they were a match; she could feel it both in her heart and in her head. Could he even love? Could she for that matter? They were both damaged. He was damaged from the Great War. She was damaged from the expectations that had been placed on her. She was like a wild mustang that had been corralled in captivity. Then there was the event that had happened earlier today with Gordon and the lion. If it hadn't been for Kagiso, Gordon would be dead now, and it would have been her fault. No use making Thomas the scapegoat; she felt she bore the responsibility. How could Gordon even begin to forgive her?

The wood had stoked the fire, and it was burning high and hot, angrily popping and spewing burning wood shards in random directions like an erupting volcano. The heat was uncomfortable against her skin, condemning her like a merciless judge. She heard sounds, almost as if coming from the fire, tormented sounds, sounds like those of the damned in hell. Were her thoughts convicting her and giving her a preview of her sentence? The sounds of torment grew in intensity, and Amelia realized they weren't coming from the fire. Instead, they were coming from Gordon's tent. He was having a nightmare. Suddenly the sounds stopped, and Amelia heard stirring inside of Gordon's tent.

Gordon opened the flap, slapping it against the canvas material, and he emerged looking like a mummy that had only been halfway wrapped in linen strips across its torso. He gingerly walked over to the log where Amelia was sitting, wincing as he attempted to sit beside her. The combination of his wrapped torso and the pain made him look as if he were an eighty-year-old man trying to stoop.

"Since the lion didn't get me, are you trying to burn the camp down now?"

Amelia assumed he was trying to make a joke, but his wincing face and clenched teeth didn't convey the levity. She didn't respond.

"Trouble sleeping?" he continued. "I can certainly imagine that you would, coming as close to death as you did today."

"You seem to be having trouble sleeping as well. Are you in pain?"

"My painkiller is wearing off." Gordon reached for the flask at his hip, trying to minimize his movement. He unscrewed the top and took a hearty drink from it. "Care for some?" he asked, offering the flask to Amelia.

"Sure." Amelia took a hearty sip herself, made a slight but quick wince, and handed the flask back to Gordon. "Kentucky bourbon must be hard to come by out here." Gordon's eyebrows rose in surprise. Amelia wasn't sure if it was because of the hearty drink she took, her toleration of the straight alcohol, or the fact that she identified the liquor.

"It is, especially considering that the United States has

Prohibition at the moment. I must say I'm impressed. You know your alcohol."

"I speak gin fluently." Amelia spoke with a velvet smokiness in her voice. "You can't beat a good gin and tonic, but I'm also pretty good with scotch or bourbon."

"I imagine that will come in quite handy after you're married, considering the future groom."

Amelia wanted to laugh at Gordon's more than likely accurate prognostication of her future with Thomas, but remembering the judgment from the fire she felt only a few moments ago, decided against laughing. A desperate urge swelled inside her to thank Gordon for risking his life, especially since she and Thomas had been so careless with the lions. She suddenly burst out, "Thank you for saving our lives." Her voice turned apologetic. "I didn't know that Thomas was going to do something that foolish. We took a gun along for protection. When he saw the lions, I couldn't stop him. He just raised the gun and fired into the air. I don't know why. He doesn't even like guns."

Gordon sighed, and Amelia could almost see past memories from the simple utterance. "I've seen it before," Gordon confessed. Gordon's face was a blank slate. Amelia thought he was casually observing those past memories. "The boyfriend or husband gets jealous and then tries to prove to his girl that he can take care of her. He forgets how dangerous it is out here and that we are professionals." Gordon came out of his trance-like state and turned his attention to Amelia. "Still, you shouldn't have gone out without Kagiso or me."

"What you did was very brave." Amelia squinted her eyes and pursed her lips in curiosity. "Why didn't you try to shoot the lion?" Amelia watched Gordon's face as he contemplated.

"I saw a lot of horrors in the Great War. I did kill the man-eaters to keep them from killing people, but I don't want to kill unless I have to."

"You could have been killed today."

"That would ease my pain." Amelia cocked her head to the side. "I don't expect you to understand that," replied Gordon in response to her gesture.

"Are your nightmares related to the war?"

Gordon hesitated before answering. "They are."

"So, what kind of gun do you have?" Amelia could tell that the question took Gordon by surprise. She wasn't sure herself why she asked it. Perhaps to take Gordon's mind off his thoughts. Of course, asking about a gun was strange when his nightmares obviously involved guns, but she was a firm believer in talking about what bothered one, rather than dancing around the topic.

"The kind that kills."

"I mean what's its make? Who designed it?

"The Devil," he answered matter-of-factly.

"I think it was man," Amelia answered just as matter-of-factly.

"I have a W.J. Jeffery 450 400 double rifle. Does that mean

anything to you?"

"Not at all. I'm going to turn in," Amelia declared abruptly.

"Why are you telling me?"

"I thought you might want to watch me as I walk away." Amelia smiled mischievously. "Good night, Gordon Powell." Amelia sashayed to the big tent and stood in front of a table holding gramophone records. She perused the stack, selected one, placed it on the gramophone, and wound the gramophone. Pops and crackling noises came through the sound horn, and soon *The Man I Love* began playing. Amelia gently swayed with an imaginary partner while Gordon stared fixedly from the log.

Chapter 11

Sarah gently closed the leather-bound diary and caressed it lovingly.

"That was so romantic," exclaimed Jill. "I wish I could have known Amelia. She must have been a fireball."

"What was romantic about a lion attack and a conversation around a campfire?" interjected Jack.

"Men!" Jill snapped back at her brother. She turned to face Sarah. "Don't stop now! What happened next?"

Sarah slumped her shoulders and dropped her head. "I don't know," she replied disappointedly. "That's all there is! The remaining pages were ripped out. Those must have been the ones that were in the box at the museum. That would make sense since that story would have taken place after what I just read."

Jill's eyes grew wide. "What? That can't be. We can't be left hanging. Look again. There has to be something else."

Sarah resolutely looked through the box again. "Other than pictures, nothing else is in here."

"Do the pictures give a clue?" asked Jill.

"I looked through all of them earlier. They all appear to be either during their safari or prior. I can't believe I've found so much but still have no clue as to what ultimately happened to change Gordon Powell."

"But you do know." Gacoki had been silent to this point. He looked over to Jill and smiled. "It was love."

Jill returned Gacoki's smile and turned to Sarah, studying her expression. "Are you alright, Sarah? You look as though something has upset you."

Sarah reluctantly pulled out the photo of her grandfather at the Powell Camp. She held it out, and the others gathered behind her to look at the photo.

Jack's eyebrows rose, and his mouth opened slightly. "This is at our camp. Who is the man in the picture?"

Sarah sighed and with a heaviness in her voice explained the photo they were seeing. "He's my grandfather. He suffered from PTSD from the Vietnam War. I was really close to him, but sometimes he seemed so distant. It hurt me to see him like that. My grandfather is one of the reasons I came here. I wanted to find out how Gordon overcame his trauma. I know you say that love was the reason that Gordon overcame his trauma, but my grandfather had love too. Was the love my grandfather had not enough? Did I not do enough for him?"

"I'm sure that's not the case." Jack draped his arm over Sarah's shoulders. "PTSD is a complex disorder. I'm sure it is highly individualized and affects everyone differently. What you're doing is admirable, but you can't blame yourself or believe that you didn't show enough love." Jack looked at the photo again. "Your grandfather looks very happy in the picture. Perhaps, as Amelia said, he felt connected to life here."

Sarah nodded, but tears streamed down her face.

"Is something else bothering you?" asked Jill.

I think being connected is part of my problem. I don't feel connected to life back in Colorado. Being here, I can understand why my grandfather seemed so happy in that picture." Sarah wiped the tears from her face. "I'm going to go back to my tent for a while. I'm worn out."

"I heard that you like learning about other cultures," interjected Gacoki. "I'm going to the village tomorrow. Perhaps you would like to come along and see our culture firsthand."

"I'd love to." Sarah forced a smile on her face. "I just may need three cups of coffee tomorrow."

Chapter 12

The jeep jostled Sarah back and forth. She wondered if she would ever get accustomed to riding in one. The movement reminded her of a similar experience from her past, that of riding a horse one time in Colorado. She pondered that with time and more experience she would become accustomed to the movement. Those who rode horses or sailed on ships eventually grew accustomed to the rhythmic movement so that it was second nature to them. "So, tell me about the Maasai Mara."

"Many still live by the old traditions." Gacoki's voice vibrated as he spoke due to the bouncing of the jeep over the road. "However, much of the land they lived on has been turned into wildlife reserves or national parks. The plans that Jill and I have would give land back to the Maasai. Then, the camp would use proceeds from our guests' reservation fees to rent the land from the Maasai."

"So, the land would be given back to the Maasai, and the camp would rent it from them." Sarah thought that was what Gacoki meant, but she rephrased it to make sure she understood. "That's an interesting concept. Tell me more."

"That's right. Wildlife conservancies and large hotel groups own a lot of land, which has changed the traditional way of life the Maasai used to live. The fences around the conservancies also prevent natural animal migration, which has led to declines in some of the animal populations."

"I didn't know that," exclaimed Sarah with surprise. "One would think animal conservancies would be a good thing." Sarah grabbed the door frame as the jeep bounced over a pothole in the road.

"As with many ideas, there are often unintended consequences. The conservancies aren't all bad; they just don't provide a panacea." As the jeep approached the village, Gacoki pointed to some dwellings. "The village is called a manyata. The dwellings or huts you see are called inkajijik huts, which are actually constructed by the Maasai women. The huts are made out of materials such as mud, cow dung, and wood. Cooking is done inside the hut. There is no electricity or indoor plumbing."

Sarah marveled at the huts.

"My grandfather lives in this village, and I come to see him at least once a month."

"What should I do while you visit your grandfather?"

"I'll introduce you to him. I haven't had a chance to ask him about Gordon Powell; so, we can ask him. Then, I'll arrange for one of the village women to show you around the village."

Gacoki pulled the jeep near a hut and parked. As Sarah exited the jeep, her legs wobbled, and she felt as though she needed to adjust to solid land again. Gacoki called out, and a man, who appeared to be in his late seventies came out to greet them and then motioned for them to enter his hut. The hut was a little smaller than those around it, and Sarah assumed it was because Gacoki's grandfather lived alone.

Coming from the bright outdoors, Sarah's eyes had trouble adjusting to the dimly lit hut. Gacoki was right, there was no electricity or electrical appliances inside the hut. The only light illuminating the hut was natural light coming in through the doorway and through small ventilation holes. There were no windows in the hut. A fireplace was in the center of the hut, and an opening in the roof of the hut allowed the smoke to escape. Although no fire was going at the moment, Sarah could smell the ghosts of fires past that were harbored in the walls of the hut. The furniture and décor were minimal; a mat on the floor served as the grandfather's bed, and animal skins were used for seating. Despite the smoky and woodsy smell, the small space was quite cozy.

"This is Sarah," Gacoki told his grandfather. "She is visiting the area to do some research."

Gacoki's grandfather said something to Gacoki in the Maa language, and Gacoki replied in Maa.

"What did he say?" asked Sarah. She thought she heard Gacoki's grandfather mention Jack's name.

"I'm sorry," replied Gacoki apologetically. "Please pardon my manners. My grandfather doesn't speak much English. He asked if you were Jack's girlfriend. I told him that you were not. He said you and Jack would make a good couple."

Sarah's mind dwelled temporarily on the thought of her and Jack as a couple before replying. "He can determine that just by seeing me?"

"He thinks he can," Gacoki answered with the mild embarrassment that one's elders sometimes cause.

"Will you ask him if he knows anything about Gordon Powell or Kagiso?"

Gacoki asked his grandfather the question in Maa.

Gacoki's grandfather turned to Sarah and replied in English, "When you have specific questions to ask, come back and see me."

Sarah was taken aback by the response. "I don't mean to be disrespectful, but why can't you tell me now?"

"When the time is right, come back."

Sarah became more frustrated at the broken-record response but maintained her patience. "How will I know when that will be?"

"You will know."

Sarah turned to Gacoki open-mouthed. "I thought you said he didn't speak much English!"

"I never spoke to him in English, except for introducing you a couple of minutes ago."

Gacoki's reply was so matter of fact that Sarah laughed. *Men*, she thought to herself. Sarah turned to Gacoki's grandfather. "Thank you for speaking with me. I'll be back." Sarah meant it and was now more determined than ever to find the rest of the pieces of the puzzle she was missing and the whole story. Gacoki's grandfather smiled broadly. Gacoki's grandfather walked Sarah and Gacoki to the door of his hut. As Sarah walked out into the bright sunlight, she had to shield her eyes, which had to readjust to the light. As she turned to wave bye to Gacoki's grandfather, the sunlight gleamed off the necklace he was wearing. The image jarred her memory, but her mind didn't immediately register what she saw. She walked several feet away before her mind identified the necklace. She turned around to look one more time to confirm what she thought she saw, but Gacoki's grandfather had already gone back inside the hut. "What was the necklace your grandfather was wearing? It looked like military dog tags. Was your grandfather in a war, or was he close to someone who was in a war?"

"I don't know. I guess I'm just used to seeing him wear them. I've never thought about it."

Sarah shook her head. "Between you and Jack, neither of you know much about your families' pasts."

"I'm going to go help my grandfather with a few things, but I've arranged for someone to show you around the village. I know that she speaks English," Gacoki smiled. Gacoki took Sarah to a Maasai village woman. "Sarah, this is Nasinka."

"That's a beautiful name. Does it have a special meaning?"

"It means shining star," answered the woman.

"That's beautiful." Sarah's insides hummed with excitement. Experiencing different cultures firsthand was what inspired her, not the mundane work of helping catalog collections, developing short paragraphs to accompany pieces, or trying to explain a culture to a group of uninterested middle school students or tourists who were in a hurry to rush through the museum as quickly as possible in order to get to the next thing on their lists.

Nasinka led Sarah past several huts, and Sarah soaked in the sight of the huts made with simple earthen materials to produce a structure suited for the purposes of the culture.

"You are about to see a Maasai ceremonial dance. It is a jumping dance called the adumu. Warriors used to do this long ago in the savanna to see if predators were around. It is a dance of strength and agility."

"The clothes everyone is wearing are so pretty."

"The wraps are called shukas. Most are red in color, but you will sometimes see blue or black and checkerboard patterns."

Several Maasai warriors began to perform the adumu dance for Sarah. About a dozen men were gathered around in a semicircle holding long wooden spears and wearing colorful beaded necklaces. The men began to chant rhythmically, and two warriors stepped out from the group and began to jump straight into the air. Their bodies were as straight as the spears they held in their hands. The group that was chanting began to bend from their knees and waists and stomp the ground in rhythm with the chants. Occasionally, one of the warriors in the group would yell a high-pitched shout. The two dancers broke away and joined the group, and another warrior came out and began to jump. After several jumps, he rejoined the group, and another warrior came out and repeated the jumping.

"Wow! They can jump really high." Sarah imagined the centuries the adumu had evolved over, allowing each new generation of warriors the opportunity and experience to perfect the dance.

Nasinka's eyes twinkled. "Everyone who sees this for the first time says the same thing. The adumu was originally a ceremony whereby young warriors perfected their strength. It served as sort of a graduation to mark them as experienced warriors. This was just one ritual dance of the Maasai. Dances were also done for celebrations, such as wedding ceremonies, or as a blessing of cattle, or other ceremonies."

All of the warriors were back in the semicircle chanting. "What's next?" shouted Sarah to be heard above the chants.

"Now, they are waiting for you to try."

"Me! I don't ..."

"Go out and give it a try. Gacoki said you wanted to experience our culture firsthand. Now is your opportunity." Nasinka put a red shuka around Sarah and put a beaded necklace over her head. She gave Sarah a gentle nudge, and Sarah reluctantly made her way toward the open space in front of the group of warriors. Her heart pounded, and she breathed quick, shallow breaths. Sarah was afraid she would only lift a few inches off the ground and be laughed at. That was her head talking. Her heart wanted to go out and try even if she made a fool of herself for doing so. Her heart quickly overruled her head and she prepared to jump as the warriors' cheers gave her a newfound confidence. The shuka and necklace helped with Sarah's confidence, and she tried to see herself in the role of a warrior. She jumped, trying to mimic the posture she had observed of the dancers. On the first jump, her heels touched the ground, and she remembered that the warriors didn't let their heels hit the ground. She was glad she wasn't holding a spear. That would have been too much to concentrate on while trying to jump. Her second jump was better, but she felt she still didn't jump very high. She continued jumping to the rhythm of the chants and felt she was getting the hang of it, even if her jumps were only a fraction of that of the Maasai warriors' jumps. Her calves began to ache, and she knew she would pay the price in the morning for her jumping. She didn't care and jumped a few more times before her calves begged to stop by clinching up from weariness. With wobbly legs, she wondered now why she wanted to get out of the jeep so badly. All she wanted to do was sit. The thought was fleeting; the cheers of the Maasai bolstered her legs, and she had an exuberant feeling of accomplishment. The warriors smiled at Sarah as Nasinka came out to congratulate her. Sarah was breathing heavily from the jumping, and her legs were letting her know they weren't happy with the experience. Sarah didn't care though. Her body could chastise her later.

"Not bad for a first try," encouraged the woman. "Let's try something that's not as physically demanding."

Sarah's legs quivered as she walked with Nasinka past several huts. Sarah wondered what the next thing would be. Nasinka had said it would not be physically demanding. As she wondered, she took in the smell of woodsy smoke. It reminded Sarah of a camping trip she had gone on in Colorado years ago.

"Here we are." Nasinka pointed to a fire where several women were cooking. Sarah thought back to the camping trip and her attempt at cooking. She had gone with a few friends, and she was elected to do the cooking. That assignment only lasted for one meal. It had taken her nearly an hour to start the fire. She cooked the meat for two hours and it was still raw on the inside. After her friends complained about being hungry, Sarah stoked the fire with several pieces of wood until it was roaring like a bonfire. It was so out of control that she couldn't take off the meat. After the fire was finally under control, the meat was burned to a crisp. At least here, she could watch someone else cook, or so she thought.

Nasinka's voice interrupted her thoughts. "The meal we are going to make is called ugali. It is made from maize flour and a pinch of salt, which is added to boiling water. It is then stirred until it becomes solid. Before we do that though, we must make a fire. One of the warriors is going to show how quickly he can start a fire. The warrior is using a wooden stick fitted into a groove on a wooden plank. One end is placed on a knife. As he rubs the stick, the heat builds up."

The warrior rapidly rubbed the stick moving his hands from the top to about two-thirds of the way down the stick. He quickly moved his hands back to the top of the stick and repeated the process. Soon, smoke issued from the stick. After a few more rubs and more smoke, a brownish-blackish small mound of ashes formed on the knife. The warrior removed the plank from the knife and transferred the ashes to a small mound of dried grass. At first, the smoke looked as though it had died. The warrior massaged the nest and gently blew until the smoke reappeared and began to escape from the top and sides of the mound of dried grass. More and more smoke rolled out and the warrior continued to blow harder. Soon, Sarah couldn't see the mound of grass for the smoke. Suddenly the smoke all but stopped, and a bright orange flame burst in its place. The warrior slid the knife under the burning grass and transferred it to another area with stone-ground wood chips and sticks. The fire caught quickly, and more wood was added to the fire.

Sarah watched as another warrior worked to make another fire. He repeated a similar process, but this time, the warrior had the small mound of dried grass on top of some dried, tall savanna grass. Once the mound caught fire, the warrior rolled the mound into the tall, dried grass. The warrior blew until the fire caught, and the broom-like grass transformed into a brightly burning torch. He carried it to a teepee-like structure of wood, catching it on fire.

Sarah was amazed at the fire-starting skills of the warriors. "I can't believe how quickly they started those fires!"

"The warriors will sometimes use dried animal dung to start a fire," added Nasinka.

One of the warriors looked over to Sarah and smiled.

"He is going to let you try it now."

Apparently, Nasinka had not shared Sarah's memories of building a fire and cooking. Still, the warriors made starting a fire look so easy. Surely, she could replicate the process. The warrior laid out the materials for Sarah to use. She placed the wooden plank on top of the knife blade and fit the stick into the groove. She mimicked the hand movement she had seen the Maasai warriors do, but the stick wobbled out of the groove. Sarah tried several times, but the stick wouldn't stay in the groove. On about the tenth attempt, she was able to keep the stick in the groove, but she couldn't move her hands as fast as the warriors had. Once her hands got about two-thirds of the way down the stick, the spinning would abruptly stop. "It looked so easy when the warriors did this, but I can't get anything going. I would starve if it were up to me to start a fire this way."

Nasinka and the warrior smiled. "At least you gave it your best try," exclaimed Nasinka.

"May I at least have a taste of the ugali?" asked Sarah, "if that is okay," she quickly added.

"Of course." Nasinka let Sarah tear off a piece, and Sarah took a bite. It was a little grainy, and Sarah thought it didn't have much of a taste to it. "Ugali is usually used to dip into a stew or to pick up pieces of vegetables or meat in a sauce. Most outsiders find it bland tasting eaten alone."

Gacoki appeared as Sarah was finishing her piece of ugali. "Are you ready to head back to the camp? I hope you had an enjoyable time with Nasinka."

"It was wonderful! I had a great time. Thank you so much, Nasinka for letting me experience your culture."

Back in the jeep on the way back to Powell Camp, Sarah thought about how enjoyable her day with the Maasai had been. "Thank you for letting me go to the village with you. I had a great time, except for trying to start a fire."

"You're very welcome. I heard that you tried the adumu. Did you enjoy it?"

"It was very fun, but I think my legs are going to be sore

tomorrow." Sarah thought a moment. "It would be great for you to incorporate a visit to the village as one of the camp's activities."

"That's what Jill and I have told Jack."

"Is he opposed?"

Gacoki reflected before answering. "I wouldn't say he is opposed. He is facing some financial struggles with the camp and doesn't want to introduce anything new at the moment."

"If what he's doing is not bringing in sufficient revenue, then he should do something different. Otherwise, he will continue getting the same results."

Gacoki laughed as he swerved around a pothole in the road. "That's what Jill and I have told him. Maybe you will have better luck trying to convince him than we have had."

As the jeep pulled up to the camp, Sarah could see Jack and Jill arguing, but she couldn't make out what they were saying over the noise of the jeep's engine. Gacoki turned off the jeep, and Sarah climbed out of the jeep. Jack and Jill stopped arguing immediately.

"Did you have a good visit?" asked Jack.

"Yes. It was wonderful to see how the Maasai Mara live. This is the kind of thing I want to do as a cultural anthropologist, not working in a museum."

"Were you able to find out anything from Gacoki's grandfather about Gordon Powell?" asked Jill.

"Not yet."

A puzzled expression came over Jill's face. "Did you not get a chance to ask him?" Jill looked at Gacoki with a stern expression on her face. "Did you not talk to your grandfather about him? You said you would ask."

Jill still seemed to be upset from what she and Jack and been arguing about, and Sarah quickly intervened before Jill transferred any residual anger to Gacoki. "I spoke with him about both Gordon and Kagiso, but his comments were very enigmatic."

"What do you mean?"

"He told me to come back when I had specific questions and that I would know when the time was right."

"That's strange," replied Jill. "I wonder why he didn't just tell you what he knew while you were there." Jill turned to face Gacoki. "Couldn't you persuade your grandfather to tell her?"

Gacoki looked down at his feet. "Grandfather can be very stubborn sometimes, but I'm sure he'll tell Sarah what he knows. Maybe Sarah needs to find out some more information first."

"That's easier said than done," exclaimed Sarah. "I've come to a dead end at the moment, but I'll keep trying to find out more. Hopefully, the boxes in the basement still contain something we just need to find."

"Is there not another source of information or avenue you can explore? I would think everything would have been in the box you found," apprised Jack. Jill looked sternly at Jack. It was a look that

Sarah interpreted as *don't burst her bubble.*

"I just need to have faith that I'll find more, either in the remaining boxes or through some means I haven't thought of yet."

Gacoki asked Jill to walk with him. Sarah speculated that that was Gacoki's way of removing her before Jill's anger surfaced again. "Is everything ok?" Sarah asked Jack. "It looked like you and Jill were arguing when we drove up."

Jack sighed, releasing the tension in his shoulders as they dropped and relaxed. "We've been doing that a lot lately. It's always about our financial situation. I'm afraid that if things don't pick up, we may have to close the camp. Unfortunately, it may be very soon. Neither one of us want to admit it, and I have no clue what we'll do if, or when, that time comes."

"It sounds like you might ought to try some new things and so some marketing." Sarah knew she was intruding in an area that wasn't her place to intrude, but she hated the idea of the camp closing, and she had come to care deeply about Jack and Jill during her short time at the camp.

"It sounds like you have been talking to Gacoki or Jill." Jack's tone thankfully wasn't one of anger, thought Sarah. "As I mentioned before," continued Jack, "I'm definitely not against any of their ideas, but all of that takes money. I'm afraid spending money on those things would put us under before we could realize any benefits from them."

"It was just an idea." Sarah proceeded cautiously in hopes of not reigniting Jack's anger. "It seems like if something is not working, then continuing the status quo would only continue the downturn."

"Are you reminding me that the definition of insanity is continuing to do the same thing but expecting different results?"

"I didn't say that." Sarah was quick to come back with her statement. She tried to tactfully finesse her way around implying that directly, but Jack had seen through it.

"You didn't have to." Jack blinked his eyes, and his gaze held out an unspoken plea. "Look, even if we did implement them, we would have additional costs. We need more guests, which would require more tents, which would require more money that a bank won't lend us."

"It all sounds very circular, but you have to start somewhere." Sarah could feel a palpable shift in the air. Jack's jaw clenched, and his nostrils flared as his face developed a slight reddish tint. His body stiffened. Sarah knew the conversation would quickly escalate into an argument. She was sure that Jack had had this same argument numerous times with Jill and that he didn't see a workable alternative to the camp's financial situation. Perhaps Jack could talk with a financial or marketing consultant to generate ideas that Jack didn't see, but Sarah wasn't about to suggest that while Jack was on the verge of erupting. All she wanted to do at the moment was deescalate the tension she could feel. "I don't want to fight with you. I'm a visitor who doesn't know the full picture. I appreciate all you've done for me."

Those simple but heartfelt words melted the tension immediately and Jack's face returned to its normal tanned color, and his breathing returned to full breaths rather than the quick, shallow breaths from a moment earlier. His shoulders relaxed once more. "I don't want to argue with you either. I've really enjoyed you being here." Jack hesitated, as if in thought. "To show you there are no hard feelings, how about having dinner with me tonight, just you and me?"

"I'd love that." Sarah's quick response to Jack's dinner offer gave her a tinge of guilt. An image of Wesley entered her mind, and she fidgeted with a nonexistent ring on the ring finger of her left hand. The image quickly faded and was replaced by an imagined dinner with Jack. Conflicting emotions swirled within her. She felt the butterflies dancing around the knot of betrayal in her stomach. "See you tonight." Sarah smiled and walked away before her eyes reflected the conflict within her.

Sarah had brought a mixture of casual and business clothes on her trip, not knowing what to expect. She did, however, bring a social dress just in case an occasion called for one. She felt that tonight qualified as one of those occasions. The dress was an open-back, midi slip with spaghetti straps in French-Blue that fell between her knees and ankles. She had a pair of sterling silver linear drop earrings with matching silver high heels. Sarah hoped she wasn't overdressing, but something inside of her told her that casual or business dress wouldn't suit her dinner with Jack. Once she had dressed, the gentle stirring of butterflies brushed her insides as she anticipated being alone with Jack. To quelch the feeling, she tried thinking of Wesley, but she couldn't hold the thought in her mind. Instead, all she could see was Jack's ruggedly handsome features.

Jack told her to meet him at a spot near the dining tent, and he would escort her from there to a private location. As Sarah exited her tent, her heartbeat quickened, and she noticed that she was rubbing her fingers together. She again hoped that she had not overdressed, but she had seen other guests dressed up at night in elegant clothes. Some of the men even wore tuxedos, which seemed surprising to her here in the African savanna. She arrived at the spot to find Jack waiting for her. Jack was dressed up as well. Seeing him in clothes other than his everyday work clothes caught her slightly off guard, even though she had expected he would wear something different. He wore a navy suit with a white shirt, sans tie, but even without the tie, Jack appeared elegantly dressed. When Jack spotted her, she could see his eyes widen and his facial muscles tense. She smiled inwardly but tried to keep her own facial expression neutral. The look in his eyes told her that he was admiring her, and she was glad that he seemed to share the same feelings she had.

"You're stunning." Jack held his bent arm for Sarah to hold.

Sarah had known Jack to be a man of few words, but the simple statement he uttered brought a smile to her face. "You clean up nicely, yourself."

"I was hoping to get a slightly different response." He almost seemed taken aback.

"You're very handsome. I just didn't want to say something that would go to your head."

"By all means, say it. I very rarely have the opportunity for my ego to be stoked."

"In your words, you're stunning, yourself. But then again, you're handsome in your everyday clothes. Now, I think your ego is stoked enough."

"It is. Enough to last me a week, at least." Jack led Sarah beyond the dining tent to a narrow path surrounded by trees. They walked slowly and silently for a few minutes. Sarah was unsure what to say, and she sensed that Jack felt the same.

Dusk would soon turn to night, but enough light was left to guide them along the path. The path ended at a clearing where Sarah could see a tent perched on a small hill. The soft glow of lanterns and candles encircled and illuminated the tent. Sarah reached the tent in time to catch the beauty of the savanna from this spot before darkness encompassed it. Jack pulled out a chair for Sarah at the cozy table for two.

As Jack reached his own chair, a waiter brought out two cocktails on a tray. "You'll have to try our specialty cocktail," announced Jack. "It's called a Safari Sunset. We're just having it after sunset."

Sarah made a pouty lip expression. "I'm sorry. I took too long getting ready. If I had arrived at our rendezvous ten minutes sooner, we would have seen the sunset."

"As beautiful as you look, you were worth the wait."

Sarah took a sip, and her face lit up, as if reflecting the candlelight. "This is very good! I'll have to remember the name of this drink for later. I assume that this is not just a special occasion drink and that I can order this at the bar."

"It's one of our regular drinks, one of our most popular ones, actually. When you finish that one, I can have him bring you another."

"I think that will be a definite possibility."

When the waiter brought out soup, Jack asked him to bring Sarah another Safari Sunset cocktail. Sarah closed her eyes and sniffed the aroma rising from the bowl of soup. When she opened them, she noticed Jack staring at her, the corners of his lips ever so slightly turned upwards.

"What?" asked Sarah. "Why are you staring at me like that?"

"Just enjoying you enjoy the soup, or at least the smell of the soup. I'm watching to see your expression when you take a sip."

"Okay." Sarah took a spoonful of soup and blew gently on it in case it was hot. Then she put the spoonful in her mouth and savored the taste before swallowing. She closed her eyes and let out a small sigh. "This is really good too. I don't think I've ever had any soup that tastes like this."

"It's a roasted butternut soup."

"Well, it tastes a lot better than it sounds."

"What do you mean," questioned Jack with a puzzled expression.

"The name just sounds like it would be fine dining for a squirrel."

Jack roared with laughter. "I've never thought of it that way, but you're right."

Almost two hours had passed as Sarah and Jack talked and laughed while they ate. They had finished their entrées and were sipping an after-dinner wine.

"When do you think you will go back to the States?"

Sarah detected a hesitancy in Jack as he asked the question. "Are you trying to get rid of me? Is this my last meal before you put me on a plane tomorrow?"

"Definitely not. I wish you would stay longer. In fact, I was thinking of hiding the diary to keep you here a while."

A sly look came over Sarah's face. "Is that your trick? You let me stay free for a week and then double the normal rate for the next week?"

"You found me out," teased Jack. "Seriously though, I'd be glad for you to stay. And don't worry about the money." He hesitated. Sarah wondered if he was thinking of something to say next so that he didn't sound too forward. "You're paying me back by giving me information about my ancestor."

"You don't have to try too hard to get me to stay longer. I love it here. Eventually, my vacation will run out, and I'll have to return to work."

Jack grew somber, as if recalling a distant memory. "Yes. I'm sure you see this as a great vacation, but vacations end, and reality eventually returns."

Sarah didn't think that Jack intentionally meant for his comment to sound like a jab, but it came across that way through his sharpened tone of voice and through the dour expression on his face. His body language also betrayed him; he had crossed his arms and turned his head away. Sarah sensed that he was thinking about his former fiancée. So, thinking of the expression she had often heard in Colorado, she decided to take the bull by the horns and confront him directly. "Not everyone is like your ex-fiancée. Being here has awakened me and makes me question what good I'm actually doing at my job at the museum."

Her directness seemed to shake Jack out of his somber mood. He uncrossed his arms and looked at her face-to-face. The tone of his voice had also lost its sharpness and sounded neutral. "You have stability in a job you don't love. I have a job I love that may not be stable. That all somehow seems ill-fated." He paused for a moment and then changed the subject. "But let's not talk about that now. How was your food?"

Sarah put down her fork. She wanted to go back to the previous subject. Why ruin a good night, though? Rather than taking the bull by the horns for a second time, she would employ another bullfighting analogy and keep the bull distracted by the matador's red cape. If he wanted to change the subject, she could dance in the moment herself. "Well, I'm full. That was really good."

"You can't be full. You have to save room for dessert. And then there is the dessert wine."

"I may be too full," Sarah reiterated.

"Nonsense. Didn't you know that your stomach has a special pocket just for dessert?"

"I didn't know you were a professor of anatomy too!" teased Sarah.

"That's common knowledge. Tell you what. Let's compromise. We can share one. Once you taste it, you'll be glad you took my advice."

"Okay." Sarah answered with a laugh. "Seeing as you're in the mode of giving advice, do you have any other advice you'd like to share?"

The wide-eyed gleam in Jack's eyes made him appear as though she had just given him an epiphany. "As a matter of fact, yes." Jack's tone of voice had changed to one of excitement, seemingly confirming the epiphany. Jack sprung from his chair and went immediately to a hand-cranked gramophone in the corner of the private dining tent. He cranked the gramophone and played a record that Sarah swore had to be an original shellac disk from the 1920s. Even before a song began to play, she could hear the familiar popping noise old records made. "Care to dance?"

Jack definitely looked debonair as he stood with his arm stretched out toward her. He reminded her of a leading man from an old 1940s movie. "I'd love to, but how is that advice?"

"Live in the moment!"

Sarah rose before her brain even acknowledged that she was moving. The way Jack said, *live in the moment*, lit a fuse of anticipation and excitement. When her hand accepted his outstretched hand, she felt a palpable spark surge through her that further accelerated the fuse until it reached the powder keg of emotion inside her. She knew then for certain that she had feelings for Jack. Her mind registered the song that was playing on the gramophone, *Stardust*. Sarah felt as though a star had exploded inside of her sending shimmering sparks of stardust throughout her being. They danced slowly beside of their table, and Jack held her close and tight against him. Sarah laid her head on Jack's shoulder. She peered into the night sky and saw a shooting star flash across the sky. She felt as though she were in a dream, and the song had called forth a star that was raining stardust on them as they danced. With her head on Jack's shoulder, she closed her eyes, and as Jack had advised, lived in that moment.

Chapter 13

The next morning, Sarah sat at a table in the dining tent and drank a cup of coffee. She thought about the dance that she and Jack shared the night before. Other guests were talking about their plans for the day while eating breakfast, but Sarah was oblivious to the conversations; she was absorbed in her own memories. Suddenly, Jack's voice interrupted her daydreams, but she was glad to see him in person and not just in her mind's eye.

"I see that you've taken a liking to Kenyan coffee."

Sarah took another sip before answering. "Yes. I think I'm becoming addicted to it. Back in Colorado, I'm not that much of a coffee drinker." Sarah took another sip. "Thank you for last night. I really had an enjoyable time, just the two of us." She suddenly felt a little awkward. What if Jack hadn't felt the same feelings she had? She changed the subject. "I'm sorry about earlier yesterday. I just felt a little down about finding so much about Gordon and Amelia but still being a long way from finding the complete story."

"There's only one thing to do when you're feeling down."

An hour later, Sarah stood in an open field in front of a hot air balloon. Sarah wondered if last night was a dream that was still continuing. Jack helped her into the basket, and soon, they were soaring high up over the savanna.

"As I said, there's only one thing to do when you're feeling down, and that is to get above it all and see it from a different perspective."

"I didn't know you meant it literally, but this is not the first time. I must keep reminding myself to take you literally when you say something."

Jack smiled. "I've always been a firm believer in saying what you mean."

"Always?" Sarah remarked as she stared into Jack's eyes.

"Well, I … Hey, look there!" Jack pointed to a herd of impalas running under the balloon.

Jack did not seem the type who was easily embarrassed, but Sarah thought that she had just succeeded in embarrassing him. She still wondered what his true feelings were toward her, but she was beginning to think that he just might feel something for her too. They were both silent for a while. Sarah wondered if Jack was unsure of what to say or if he was in the moment, enjoying the time they were having together. Occasionally, Jack pointed out different animals to Sarah as they flew over the savanna.

The expanse lay before Sarah like a living canvas with herds of animals coursing through the patchwork colored with various hues of golds, browns, and greens. It seemed to go on forever. An occasional breeze greeted Sarah's face, jostling her hair. The experience in the hot air balloon was much different than that of the traditional jeep safari. She liked both experiences; the hot air balloon, as Jack previously indicated, offered a different perspective. The land safari offered up-close views of the animals, but the hot air balloon provided a sense of peace. The balloon suddenly rose higher, and Sarah experienced a sensation of weightlessness. Even suspended high above the savanna, Sarah still felt a connection with the savanna below. She had never been in a balloon before, but this would be an experience she knew she would never forget.

"Is this available to all of your guests?" asked Sarah, loudly. The breeze, the altitude, or perhaps a combination of the two created a condition whereby Sarah had to shout to be heard.

Jack had to raise his voice level as well. "No, but it's definitely a good idea. The only problem is that every new thing involves a cost, which is difficult for us to do at the moment."

"Are you really in that bad of shape?"

"At the rate we're going, we may have to close before much longer."

"Are you sure a bank won't lend you the money?"

"Not with the shape we're in, and we already have a loan." Jack paused for a moment, as if reflecting. "Hmph." The sound that Jack made wasn't exactly a laugh. Sarah thought it was more a scoff, sarcastic, or insincere laugh. "It's funny about banks; they generally will only lend money when they are guaranteed to get it back."

"Could you sell some of your land?" pondered Sarah aloud.

"It's already collateral for our current loan. Let's enjoy the view. This balloon ride is supposed to lift spirits. We'll begin our descent soon. Hey," asked Jack abruptly, "do you have plans tonight?"

"Sure, I thought I would hop in the car and go shopping somewhere." The sarcasm of Sarah's reply caught her attention fully when she noticed the serious expression on Jack's face. "No, I don't have plans tonight."

"Good. I want to show you something."

The excitement that Sarah felt earlier returned. Was tonight going to be a second date? Was last night even a first date? She thought Jack had feelings for her, or was he just being nice? Maybe tonight would tell her more.

Sarah dressed casually. She hoped that was the right choice. She didn't feel it appropriate to wear what she wore last night, and she had already had dinner.

"Sarah? Are you in there?"

"I'll be right out."

"You look beautiful," Jack declared as Sarah exited her tent. "Come take a walk with me." Jack carried a lantern to illuminate their path as they walked.

Sarah was unsure of the direction they were heading, and she had lost track of the time they had spent walking. She also wondered what Jack had planned. They had been walking on level ground, but now they were treading up a small hill similar to the one they had had dinner on the previous night. This was a different hill though. Sarah was used to the Colorado altitude; so, this was an easy climb for her. When they reached the top of the hill, Sarah looked around. She didn't know what she was expecting to see, but she didn't see anything, not even an acacia tree. She was puzzled and looked at Jack who wore an expressionless face. "So, what did you want to show me?" She was curious, and the pitch in her voice had risen a little higher than normal.

"This," beamed Jack.

"This?" The pitch in Sarah's voice had risen even higher. She opened her eyes wider, as if letting in more light would let her see what Jack apparently saw, but all she saw was darkness enveloping them like a thick blanket. She looked at Jack, but he had extinguished the lantern. She thought she could make out a sly smile, but she wasn't sure. She could barely see his face much less his mouth.

"Yes. Look up!" Jack moved his head in an upward motion, and Sarah followed with her eyes.

It took her a few seconds to realize what Jack had wanted her to see, but it suddenly dawned on her. The sky was filled with stars. The stars dotted the celestial canvas like diamonds. She had seen stars in the Colorado mountains, but she had never seen this many stars in the sky before. "Wow! I've never seen so many stars. You know. I haven't even noticed this since I've been here."

"You just have to look up!" Jack took Sarah's hand, and she could feel the electricity course through her. "Follow me." They walked a short distance, and Sarah saw a telescope that had been set up. Sarah's insides tingled at the thought that Jack had taken the time to set up a telescope just for this event. The telescope was expensive looking; so, she knew this didn't normally sit out on the hilltop. Jack had taken a lot of time and care to show the starry night to Sarah. For that matter, Jack had spent a lot of time the night before setting up their dinner date. "Try looking through here."

Sarah looked through the eyepiece. Jack had positioned the telescope at a particular cluster of stars. "Wow! This is amazing."

"You can see lots of stars and constellations here." Sarah looked up from the telescope toward Jack, who was looking at the night sky. He turned back to Sarah and began pointing toward various constellations. "Ophiuchus, Draco, and the Southern Cross. There is Alpha Centauri." Sarah tried to follow Jack's finger as he pointed out the constellations and stars. Then she looked at Jack and marveled at his excitement at showing her the stars. Sarah's eyes had adjusted to the night sky, and she focused on Jack's face. She marveled at how handsome he was, and she couldn't turn her head away. This was a once in a lifetime opportunity to see constellations she couldn't see in Colorado, but all she wanted to do was to look at Jack.

Jack was smiling as he looked away from the night sky. Jack met Sarah's eyes. Sarah knew she was staring, but she couldn't stop. Jack looked deeply into Sarah's eyes, and he leaned in toward Sarah. His eyes were magnetic, drawing Sarah toward him. Just as they were about to kiss, Sarah was startled by the sound of an animal.

"That's a hyena," remarked Jack. "You don't need to worry. It's a long way from here."

The whooping sound of the hyena had broken the spell that

Sarah was under. The distant sound had somehow reminded her of the physical distance between Wesley and her. She suddenly felt guilty over her feelings for Jack. "It's getting late." The statement came almost involuntarily from Sarah. She immediately regretted saying it, but she felt conflicted in her emotions. Wesley didn't deserve her betrayal. They had been together for years. And yet, she had experienced stronger feelings for Jack than she had for Wesley. Yet, there was something to be said for consistency and constancy, which was Wesley's strong suit. The internal conflict raging within her mind was suddenly interrupted.

"Yeah. I suppose we had better turn in. I have an early day tomorrow."

The smile on Jack's face had disappeared. The longing look in his eyes was replaced by disappointment. Sarah's suspicion, that tonight would show her whether or not Jack had feelings for her, had been verified. She was sure that Jack had feelings for her. Matters were truly complicated.

Jack lit the lantern and led Sarah back to the camp. Sarah headed for her tent, stopped, and turned around. "Thank you for such a wonderful day."

"Anytime."

Sarah walked away. She looked briefly over her shoulder, but Jack had already disappeared.

Chapter 14

Jill wore a sly smile, and her eyes gleamed mischievously. "So, you took Sarah on a hot air balloon ride over the savanna and stargazing later?"

"I thought it would lift her spirits. Get it? Lift?"

"I get it. Dad jokes are not a good look for you. I think I like you better when you're brooding."

"I don't brood."

"Seriously? That's all you've done since *she who must not be named* broke your heart. I'm glad you're doing better. Your change of spirit seems to coincide with Sarah being here."

"For one thing, she has a boyfriend. For the second thing, I don't fall for guests."

"The last one is your rule. You could drop it anytime you want."

"There's still the first thing."

"I don't think either of you were thinking about her boyfriend the other night."

Jack's eyebrows lowered, causing his eyes to squint slightly. "What are you talking about?"

"Oh, come now." Jill put her hand on her hip, tilted her head, and looked wide eyed at her brother. "You didn't really think your date with Sarah was secret, did you?"

Jack shook his head from side to side in an exasperated manner. "It wasn't a date," he protested. "It was just a candlelight dinner and some dancing."

"So, … a date." Jill's head lowered and tilted, and her eyebrows arched. The corners of her lips turned up slightly. "Stop justifying. Go tell her how you feel."

"I don't know what you're talking about."

Jill repeated her previous mannerisms and in addition put her hand on her hip. "Yes, you do. You like her. You're my brother. I can read you. Admit it. You like her. Now, go do something about it. Go! Go tell her how you feel."

"I can't hide anything from you, can I."

"No, you can't. You never could."

"Even if you're right, I don't know that it would do any good."

"It may not, but it also may. Go. Go!"

Jack sighed, his shoulders relaxed, and he conceded. "Alright."

Jack walked out of the staff lodge and began to head to Sarah's tent. Gacoki drove up by the dining tent with several new guests in the jeep. Jack looked in the direction of Sarah's tent and then back to the jeep. He sighed and walked down to greet the newly arrived guests. Jill came up from behind him.

"Why don't you go talk to Sarah? I'll greet the new guests."

"This won't take long."

"Quit procrastinating."

"I'm not. I'm just doing my job. I'll talk with her as soon as we greet the new guests."

Jack and Jill greeted each new guest as they exited the jeep, welcoming them to the camp. They directed them to the social tent to have a drink before getting them settled into their tents. Jack did a double take as the last guest began to step down from the jeep. He whispered to Jill. "Is he wearing a pith helmet? Jill chuckled. Jack knew they were both recalling the entry from Amelia's diary of Thomas coming out of his tent in a pith helmet and wearing a sidearm. Although the other guests were tired but happy, this guest looked as though he would rather be any place else other than at the camp.

"Excuse me," the man said as he awkwardly stepped from the jeep, almost falling. Both Jack and Jill grabbed him before he fell on his face. The man didn't thank them for helping him. He seemed as though he didn't even realize he would have fallen if not for their help. "Could you tell me where I could find Sarah Jacobs? I'm her boyfriend Wesley."

"Wesley?" Jack knew the voice and turned around to see Sarah standing behind him. "What are you doing here?"

Wesley straightened his pith helmet, and Jack noticed Sarah biting her lip and trying her best to stifle a chuckle. No doubt she was also recalling the entry in Amelia's diary. "I've never seen you this interested in anything," Wesley commented. "You've barely spoken to me since you've been gone, and you haven't said anything about returning." A huge smile erupted on Wesley's face. Up to this point, Jack wondered if Wesley knew how to smile. "I thought I would surprise you and also see what has you so captivated."

Sarah's mouth opened but no words came out. She rubbed the bottom of her earlobe. "I ... uh." She walked up and hugged Wesley. The hug seemed awkward to Jack, and he noticed that Wesley did not hug her in return. "I think I've reached a dead end on my investigation."

Jack thought that that was an odd first statement, after her initial surprise of seeing Wesley, to make to a boyfriend who had come all this way to see her.

Wesley straightened his shoulders, causing his chest to puff out. "Well, it so happens that I am an investigative reporter. Maybe I can help."

Jack was equally surprised that that was one of the first things Wesley would say to his girlfriend. Jack's insides churned over Wesley's braggadocious posture and tone. Jill must have felt similarly. She grasped Jack's arm firmly. He didn't know if this was for his support or as a physical outlet for her own irritation.

"Oh, Wesley. Let me introduce you to Jack and Jill Powell. He and his sister run the camp. They are descendants of Gordon Powell. Jack, Jill, this is my boyfriend, Wesley Baldwin. Wesley is a reporter."

Jack shook Wesley's hand. "Pleased to me you, Wesley."

Wesley looked around briefly. "You have a very nice setup here. It looks a little colonial. Do you get any pushback on that?"

Jack noticed that Sarah bit her lip at Wesley's comment. She shot a glance toward Wesley, but he didn't see it. Jack burned inside at Wesley's comment. The comment itself was not what angered Jack. He, himself, acknowledged the colonial look of the camp. Something about Wesley's tone and mannerisms angered Jack. The corner of Wesley's lip was pulled up and back on one side, either a look of contempt or a sardonic smile. He wore it with such ease. Jack could almost hear the disparagement in Wesley's voice. Jack didn't want to sound defensive. He purposely tried to sound calm and professional and simply address Wesley's comment. "This type of yesteryear style is popular with guests, but we do our best to educate them on the effects that colonialism had on the culture."

"Is that so?" replied Wesley.

"Now, if you'll excuse me, I have some business to attend to. Someone will show you to your tent momentarily." Jack turned and walked off. Once his back was turned, Jack clenched his teeth tightly and balled his fists. He could feel the heat in his face.

"Wesley, that was rude!"

"I've always been a firm believer in the saying: if it looks like a duck, quacks like a duck, and swims like a duck, then it is probably a duck. Besides, as a journalist, I pride myself in telling the truth, even if it hurts.

Sarah folded her arms, tapped her foot, and, with narrowed eyes, looked directly into Wesley's eyes. "As a journalist, I would think you would find out the story before reporting it." Sarah knew her tone was scolding, but she wanted to get Wesley's attention and let him know she wasn't happy with his behavior.

"Well, you do have a point. I've been told by my editor that I get the facts; I just need to incorporate more personal stories in my writing to show heart."

Sarah didn't know if that was Wesley's way of apologizing, but to her, her reprimand seemingly didn't register completely.

"Have you been enjoying your research here?" added Wesley.

"Definitely. I feel like I have more of a purpose when I'm doing this kind of work than I do working at the museum." Sarah noticed that Wesley was looking around as she talked.

"I'm famished. There's not a fast-food restaurant near here, is there?"

"No. I'm afraid not, but the food here is great. Let's go get you something. By the way, why are you wearing that pith helmet?"

"I got it in Nairobi from a street vendor. He said that if I was coming to the savanna, I needed the proper hat. I haven't noticed anyone else with one though. I guess I'm the only one who came prepared."

The next day, Sarah and Wesley stood behind the dining tent as Wesley tried to get a signal on his phone. Sarah's shoulders were hunched, and her arms were folded. Jack walked up as Wesley held his phone in the air and moved it around to try to see if that would get him a signal.

"Sarah," called Jack.

Sarah lifted her head and smiled. "Good morning, Jack."

"I think you will find this a good morning, indeed. I decided to look through the rest of the boxes, and I found another box with some more information about Gordon Powell."

"Really?" Sarah became fully alert and immediately straightened her posture.

"Do you want to come look at it?"

"Well, of course. Wesley, do you want to come and see it with me?"

After a few seconds of arm waving with his phone, Wesley seemed to register that his name had been spoken. "What? Oh, you go ahead. I'll try to join you shortly. I'm putting the finishing touches on my next article."

Sarah headed quickly to the staff lodge with Jack almost running to catch up to her. Wesley turned back to his arm waving, trying to find an elusive signal. Sarah slowed down, realizing that she couldn't see anything without Jack showing her the box he found. Jack caught up and they continued to the staff lodge and down to the basement.

"This is the small box I found. It has another diary from Amelia along with some other materials, but I didn't want to look too much before you had a chance to go through it."

With puppy dog eyes, Sarah looked up at Jack. "You continued going through these for me?"

Jack looked down at his shoes as he spoke. "You seemed really down. I knew we hadn't looked through all of the boxes. I was hopeful that there would be some more information."

"Thank you, Jack." Sarah put her hand on Jack's arm. She immediately felt the familiar feeling of butterflies in her stomach. "You've been really good to me."

Jack looked up from his shoes and into Sarah's eyes. "I was going to tell you about how I felt the other night."

"Really?" Sarah grew excited and the butterflies flew even faster in her stomach. Was he really going to tell her what she hoped he would … that he cared for her? Sarah knew she should feel guilty, especially since Wesley had come to Kenya, but she didn't care. Jack seemed as though he was having difficulty telling her what he felt. She wanted to urge him to tell her; so, she asked, "What was that?"

Jack's eyes were wide, and he looked off to the side. "Oh, uh … uh, just that I was really surprised that the old gramophone still worked."

Sarah felt her insides drop. She knew the disappointment had to show on her face. If Jack would just look at her, he would see it, and maybe that would give him the confidence to tell her what she wanted to hear. Sarah was about to reach up and pull his face toward hers so that he could see the disappointment for himself when she heard footsteps thumping down the stairs. She looked over to see Jill and Gacoki hurrying to meet them.

"I heard that Jack found another box with more information." Jill seemed almost excited as Sarah was herself about the news. Jill's eyes were gleaming, even in the dark basement, and Jill smiled even as she spoke. "I'm so excited. I can't wait to find out what happened after the last diary entry."

Jack had seemed to return to normal, and even though Sarah had been disappointed that Jack didn't tell her what she wanted to hear, she couldn't stay disappointed when new information about Gordon Powell and Amelia had been discovered.

Jack handed Sarah another diary with a leather cover identical to the first diary. Sarah fumbled as she opened the diary. She immediately began reading.

Chapter 15

The sun was just beginning to peek over the horizon, and Amelia was frantically searching for Gordon. Today was the last day the group would be in Kenya. They would be leaving before noon. Even now, their belongings were beginning to be loaded into trucks. Amelia saw Kagiso and ran to him. She clutched his arm gripping it so tightly that Kagiso winced. "I've been looking for Gordon everywhere." Amelia pleaded, something she never remembered doing before." I want to talk with him before we all leave. Have you seen him?"

Kagiso turned his head to the side and looked at the ground. "Uh … I'm not sure."

Amelia knew that Kagiso knew where Gordon was but had either been told by Gordon not to tell her or was unsure whether or not to tell her. She wouldn't abide hesitancy right now. The need to see Gordon was urgent. "I would play poker with you any day, Kagiso. You don't have a good poker face. Out with it. Where is he?"

The urgency in her voice pulled Kagiso's head to her and jolted him from any secrets he may have planned to keep to himself. "He didn't want me to tell you, but I think it's in everyone's best interests if I do. Gordon is in love with you. He said you've helped him see he has something to live for, but he couldn't stand to see you leave with your fiancé. He left this morning before dawn to go to Tanganyika to take a group on a safari."

Amelia's heart felt as though it had shattered into a million pieces. She was dumbfounded and could barely speak. Tears welled in her eyes, but she was determined not to let them roll down her cheek. Disappointment and desperation coated her words. "He left without saying goodbye?" A hot fury welled within her, instantly drying her eyes. The disappointment she felt a moment earlier had been replaced by sheer anger. "To be so brave against wild animals, he couldn't stay to tell a woman goodbye?" Her words were clipped and forceful.

Kagiso hung his head, but then he lifted it and met Amelia's eyes. Pleading was in his voice just as it had been in Amelia's a moment earlier. "Don't blame him for leaving. He has faced much loss. What good would it serve him to see you leave with Thomas?"

"Maybe he would have stopped me from leaving."

"Maybe you should stop you from leaving."

"Kagiso is right you know." Both Amelia and Kagiso were startled to hear Anthony's voice. Anthony had arrived to hear the tail end of the conversation. "Only you can do that. You care for Gordon, don't you?"

Amelia abandoned any pretense of propriety. Her voice was

forceful and direct. Her face was flush, her chin jutted out, her eyes were squinted, and she was leaning in as if ready to do battle. "I do, even though it's not what you and our parents want. I can't imagine a life with Thomas. I would trade my life for one day with Gordon even if I were promised fifty more years of riches and prestige with Thomas."

Anthony remained calm as Amelia railed against the expectations that had been set for her. As Amelia took a breath to continue, Anthony interjected. "I can't imagine you with Thomas either. It would be like taking a wild horse and keeping it in a stall for the rest of its life. Gordon and Kagiso saved my life. They saved your life. Neither of us would be around to have the titles we have or eventually might have if not for them. You don't need to marry someone with whom you'll be miserable. Stay with Gordon. I'll manage the fallout. It will be major, but it will pass." Anthony lowered his head and kissed the top of Amelia's head. "Take care of yourself, and take care of Gordon. I know he will take care of you."

Anthony's words defused Amelia completely. Her clenched jaw had dropped open and her squinted eyes were now wide open. Her voice conveyed shock. "I can't believe you're saying this."

Anthony placed his hands on Amelia's shoulders and looked directly into her eyes. "I may not be able to repay Kagiso for saving my life, but I can at least save Gordon and you."

"I can't thank you enough," replied Amelia with sincerity. True to her playful nature though, a mischievous smile appeared on her face. "You know I was the one who broke your bicycle and lost your favorite marbles."

Anthony snickered slightly through his nose and shook his head. "I know."

"Even after that, you're still doing this for me?"

"Yes. Besides, I got even with you by throwing away your doll."

"You did me a favor. I didn't like dolls anyway," Amelia deadpanned.

Anthony smiled but quickly grew serious. "Go, before Thomas finds out you're leaving and causes an even bigger scene. I love you, Amelia."

Amelia smiled. "I love you, brother."

At a safari camp in Tanganyika, Gordon Powell was talking with the client who had hired him. The man was in his forties. He was slim and in good physical condition. He was also very wealthy.

"I know this is a sightseeing safari, but could I persuade you to help us do some hunting?" asked the client.

"I don't do that," answered Gordon.

"I'll double the amount we discussed. Who's going to give you a better deal than me?" responded the client.

"That would be me," came the voice of Amelia as she strolled out from some nearby trees. The client simply threw up his hands and walked off.

"Amelia!" cried Gordon. "What are you doing here? You came here by yourself? How did you even find me?"

"I picked up some tracking tips these past two weeks. You're not getting rid of me that easily."

"What about Thomas?" Gordon had tilted his head, and his forehead was creased in confusion.

"He is rid of me that easily. After meeting you, I realized that I could never marry him." Amelia lifted her head upward at an angle and rubbed her chin in thought. "Actually, I realized that a long time ago, but now I'm ready to do something about it." Amelia leaned in and pressed her chest against Gordon's. She put her arms around his neck and clasped her fingers together. Amelia grew serious. "If you'll have me, you won't have the life you thought, but you'll have one full of love and adventure."

"Here's your answer." Gordon put one hand at the small of Amelia's back and the other on her shoulder blades. He pressed her hard against his body. Amelia framed his face with her hands, and they leaned in and kissed passionately.

Chapter 16

Sarah stopped reading as the entry ended abruptly. "This is the part I wanted to find out." Sarah looked to Jack. "By the way, what or where is Tanganyika?"

"It was part of what is now Tanzania," replied Jack.

"How much more is in the diary?" asked Jill excitedly.

Sarah quickly thumbed through the diary, stopping briefly on two occasions to briefly skim a paragraph. "There's not much more in the diary. She even wrote on one page that she didn't write much after this. She said she wrote in her diary to express herself since others didn't accept her as she was. Once she met Gordon, she lived life to the fullest and that was expression enough."

Sarah heard the footsteps of someone descending the stairway to the basement. She looked up and saw that it was Wesley. She flipped through a few more pages in the diary. She would go through it in more detail later, but she wanted to see if anything important stood out while everyone was gathered. "There is an interesting note in the diary. Amelia says when she and Gordon got back to the camp, Kagiso was gone. He didn't leave a note or anything, but there was a mysterious circumstance that she didn't want to think about that would affect all of their lives."

Jill pondered a moment and then offered an explanation. "Maybe Kagiso had stayed with Gordon to help him deal with his demons from the war. Once Gordon and Amelia fell in love, Kagiso probably felt that he had helped Gordon all he could and that would be fine being with Amelia."

Wesley spoke up at hearing Jill's conjecture. "My reporter instinct suggests there is more to the story than that. She said there was something she didn't want to think about that would affect all their lives. Maybe I can do some digging to find out what this mystery was."

Sarah silently read some more of the diary. "It looks like Gordon and Amelia lived on the Kenyan coast for a couple of years. Amelia says that Gordon found a new lease on life. He was able to forgive himself for the death of his brother, and he was able to put the war behind him."

"What else is in the box?" coaxed Jill.

Sarah rummaged through the box. "There are several pictures." She pulled them out and handed some to Jill and some to Jack.

"These pictures are pretty old. They look to be when they first started the camp, but I can't tell if it's this location or another location before they moved here," pronounced Jill.

"Here's one with Gordon and Amelia at the waterfall; so, it probably our current location, although it's hard to tell from the other photos. I'm sure the landscape changed somewhat over the years." Jack paused when he came to one photo, examining it closely. "I remember this one from when I was a boy." He held it up for Jill to see.

"I remember that too."

"This photo used to be in a frame that was hung in the old social tent when we were kids. It's a picture of Gordon and Amelia posing beside of the sign that says *Powell's African Camp and Safari*. I had forgotten all about this photo until now."

"We should reframe it and hang it in the social tent," exclaimed Jill.

"While we still have a camp," muttered Jack.

Sarah noticed that Jill gave Jack a reprimanding look, one that seemed to shout, *Don't say things like that in front of Wesley.*

Sarah saw that after removing the pictures, only a bulky envelope remained. Sarah pulled it and looked to Jack and then Jill as if seeking permission to open it.

Jill was the first to reply. "Well, what are you waiting for? Open it already."

Sarah tugged on the envelope flap. The adhesive was old, and the envelope opened without a tear. Sarah tilted the envelope and let the contents pour out onto an empty shelf in a shelving unit. Everyone gathered close to get a good view of what had been stored in the envelope.

"Those are old World War I military medals and badges," informed Wesley. "They definitely match what Gordon would have received." Wesley pointed at each one and described what it was. "He had two U.S. Army marksman badges, although most would refer to them as medals. The rifle expert medal shows two Springfield rifles crossed over a wreath of laurel leaves, and the pistol expert medal shows two Colt revolvers crossed on top of a wreath of laurel leaves. This is the French Croix de Guerre, a cross pattée overlaid on crossed swords, and this one with the eagle on a cross is the U.S. Distinguished Service Cross."

"How do you know so much about these?" asked Sarah.

"The marksmanship badges have the names on them telling what they are," quipped Jack.

Wesley seemed unaffected by Jack's quip. "I interviewed an army colonel for a Memorial Day article one time, and he droned on and on for over an hour about the history of army badges and medals."

After looking at the military awards, Jack, Jill, and Gacoki returned to their chairs. Sarah remained standing while Wesley leaned against a shelving unit and looked at his phone.

Sarah looked over to Jack. "Thank you, Jack, for continuing to search. This ties up a lot of loose ends, even though it creates some new ones. How can I ever repay you?"

Jack appeared nervous to Sarah. He avoided looking at her, and he seemed fidgety. While he was sitting, he rubbed the tops of his legs with his palms. Although his back was straight, his posture looked tense. "You already have repaid me. You have helped to redeem my great grandfather in my eyes. Now, why don't you and Wesley do something fun?"

"Maybe tomorrow," replied Wesley. "I want to work some more today on my article."

Gacoki, who had been quiet up to this point, raised a question. "Sarah, you said this ties up a lot of loose ends for you, but does it really?" All of this started because you wanted to know what allowed Gordon Powell to get past his PTSD. I mentioned before that love was what helped him. That's when you told us about your grandfather and how he suffered from PTSD. Do you have the answer now, and if you do, are you satisfied with the end of the story?"

Sarah's face was emotionless, but behind it, she was thinking about what Gacoki had said and asked. An overwhelming feeling of sadness washed over her like a wave on the beach washing over a shell. Tears streamed from her eyes, and she sobbed. She tried to keep herself from making a noise as she cried, but she couldn't. Gacoki looked embarrassed and probably wondered why he chose to ask the question.

Wesley walked over and put his hand on her shoulder. "Sarah, what's wrong?"

"If love is really what brought Gordon out of his PTSD, then what does that mean for my grandfather? Does that mean he didn't have enough love? Was my love and my grandmother's love for him not enough? Did we not love enough?"

Wesley spoke in a soft, calm, and confident-sounding voice that provided a soothing effect on Sarah. "Sarah, there's not a simple answer. People are different, and what works for one may not work for another. Don't question whether you loved enough. I'm sure your grandfather felt loved. You're a loving person." Wesley continued to rub and gently squeeze Sarah's shoulder until she stopped crying.

Once Sarah had stopped crying, Jack spoke up. "I may have an answer; it may not be right, but I think it is."

Sarah looked over to Jack. Her eyes were red from crying, and she was breathing through her mouth because the crying had stopped up her nose. She knew she must appear a mess, but if there was a truthful answer that would make her feel better, she wanted to hear it.

"The day after you arrived at camp, you read Jill and I the pages from the diary that had been ripped out. In those pages, Gordon said that the only time he felt alive was when he was facing danger or death. Amelia said that the danger didn't make him feel alive. Being connected was what made him feel alive. You said yourself how content your grandfather looked in the picture of him at this camp. I think that was because he felt connected here. As Wesley said, people are different. We don't know what made your grandfather feel connected here. It could have been something that someone else would care nothing about. I think Gordon felt a connection with Amelia that made him feel alive again. That doesn't mean your grandfather and grandmother loved each other less than Gordon and Amelia did, and it doesn't mean that your love for your grandfather and his for you was not strong enough. In fact, the love could have been stronger. But Gordon and Amelia connected in some way that brought life forth from a damaged soul. I think it was that their personalities were so different that they challenged each other, and like a magnet and steel, they connected."

"Thank you, Wesley. Thank you, Jack," sniffed Sarah as she rubbed her fingers under her eyes to wipe away any remaining wetness. "That does make me feel better."

"I'm sorry," interjected Gacoki as he looked at Sarah sheepishly. "I didn't mean to upset you. Please forgive me."

"There's nothing to forgive you for," replied Sarah. "I needed to address that. If I didn't address it today, it might have come up at a time when I didn't have such dear friends around to comfort me."

In the dining tent that night, Wesley had brought the article he was working on with him. He completely tuned out the conversations of other guests at nearby tables and had apparently ignored the smells of the food. He had a bowl of soup in front of him from which he occasionally took a spoonful without looking up from his work. Sarah wondered why he went to the trouble of coming all this way if he was going to continue working the whole trip. She tried to think of some things he might enjoy doing, but everything she thought of just didn't seem a good match for Wesley. Rather than continuing to guess, she finally came to the conclusion that she just needed to ask him directly. "Is there anything special you would like to do while you're here? We could go on the safari trip tomorrow." She smiled, hoping that might offer some encouragement to Wesley, but he continued to look down at the article he was concentrating on.

"I've already seen those kinds of animals in the zoo. Besides, it will probably be hot and dusty, and we'll be in some jeep all cooped up like chickens. I think I'll just stay in tomorrow to try to put the finishing touches on my article. You go without me."

"If you're sure." At least Wesley was listening, even if he weren't engaging with her. Still, she was bothered by the lack of attention. This wasn't new behavior for Wesley, but it seemed to bother Sarah more now than it had before. She wasn't sure why. Well, she did have a good idea why. She had feelings for Jack, and those feelings were calling into question everything she thought she felt for Wesley. But no one was perfect. Wesley had some issues, but he probably thought the same about her. He had come all the way to Africa because he was concerned about her. He had always been supportive of her; he was there for her. And what about Jack? His main focus was on keeping the camp solvent. In terms of Maslow's Hierarchy, his attention was on basic needs. He had to meet these needs before he could address the more psychological needs, such as love. What if he did lose the camp? Where would he go? If she were to make a list of pros and cons, not too many checks would be on the pro side for choosing Jack. Love might be the only item on the pro side of the list. But love carries a lot of weight. All you need is love according to the Beatles song. But is love all you really need? If she chose Jack, she would either have to deal with a long-distance relationship or a potentially homeless situation. Of course, the assumption in all of this was that Jack loved her, which might not be a valid assumption at all. If he didn't love her, then this pro and con exercise would be a total waste of time. And was she just experiencing an infatuation with Jack that would ultimately play itself out? Everything was so confusing. Her head was hurting thinking about it. She just needed to stop thinking. Things would work out the way they were supposed to. Maybe the answer was to leave and just go back to Colorado.

There was still a mystery to solve involving Gordon and Amelia, but she had discovered about all she was going to discover. The mystery might just have to remain a mystery.

🐘 🐘 🐘

From the other end of the dining tent, Jack and Jill focused their attention on Sarah and Wesley.

"You know it's still not too late to tell Sarah how you feel about her. You should have told her when you said you were going to," goaded Jill.

"It doesn't really matter now with her boyfriend here," replied Jack.

"Anyone can tell within one minute that they aren't suited for each other," continued Jill. "He may be a decent guy, but they don't match well."

"You really could tell that within the first minute of seeing them together. Isn't that a little judgmental? What are you basing your opinion on?"

"First impressions are usually right. Your gut will tell you if you just listen."

"Whether they're right for each other or not, they're together."

"As Amelia said in her diary, how can you be so brave yet so chicken to tell her how you feel?"

"I think you're taking too much liberty in your summary of what was in Amelia's diary."

"Maybe so, but you can still tell her."

"Oh, you just want me to walk over there right now with Wesley sitting there and tell her I love her?"

"Why not? He wouldn't even notice," deadpanned Jill.

Jack snickered. "You probably are right about that. I missed my opportunity though; it was probably for the best, I imagine. It saved me a lot of embarrassment."

"You are the most stubborn man I've ever known."

"We're twins; you're as stubborn as I am."

"We're not identical twins."

"In stubbornness we are," kidded Jack.

Jill put her hand on Jack's arm. "Just don't let stubbornness ruin your life."

Chapter 17

Sarah waited by the jeep with the other guests who were going on the safari. Everyone, except for her, had at least one other person going with them. Things like this usually didn't bother her, but today, she felt awkward. She imagined others looking at her and feeling sorry for her that she was alone. Why would Wesly come all this way just to ignore her? As she was pondering this question, Gacoki walked up.

"Ok. Everyone, climb into the jeep. I will be your guide today on the safari."

"Where's Jack?" asked Sarah. Doesn't he usually guide these tours?" The thought that Jack would lead the safari was the only consolation Sarah had.

"He does, but he said he wasn't feeling well today; so, I'm going to do it today. Sorry to disappoint you."

Sarah frowned.

"My driving isn't that bad," Gacoki joked.

"No. I didn't mean to imply it was."

Gacoki sighed, and a frown formed on his face. "You and Jack should talk. I think it's obvious to everyone but you and him that you both like each other."

"What? No. I was just curious." Sarah could feel the heat on her flushed face.

Gacoki's eyebrows rose, pulling up one corner of his lip and giving a look of incredulity to his face. "Do you not see the parallels between you and Amelia and Jack and Gordon?"

Sarah's head tilted, and she drew her eyebrows together. "What do you mean?"

"Both Jack and Gordon lost their parents when they were teenagers. Jack is going through the motions of life just as Gordon was. Gordon had Kagiso, and Jack has Jill to watch over him. Amelia wanted something different for her life, something exciting, and so do you. Amelia came into Gordon's life and made it better, just as you are doing for Jack."

"So? … There are some similarities. That doesn't mean that Jack and I like each other. I have a boyfriend."

"Precisely. He is like Thomas from Lady Amelia's diary."

Sarah rolled her eyes. "Wesley is a lot nicer than Thomas. Thomas was a complete jerk."

"True, but just as Thomas wasn't right for Amelia, Wesley is not right for you."

Sarah sighed. "I give up. Let's just go." Sarah climbed in the jeep. Everyone else was already seated.

🐘 🐘 🐘

As the jeep drove away, Wesley stepped out from behind a tent that was only a few feet from where Sarah and Gacoki were talking. He stared, tight lipped with crossed arms, watching the dusty haze given off by the jeep as it sped toward the horizon.

🐘 🐘 🐘

Later that afternoon, the safari group arrived back at camp. The day had grown hot, and the returning guests were weary. Hair had fallen due to the humidity, and everyone's clothes were wet to some extent from perspiration. Since Sarah was the last one to get into the jeep, she was the first one out. She had grown more accustomed to the jeep rides; so, this one had not taken a huge toll on her. She spotted Wesley right away and headed toward him.

"How was the safari?" asked Wesley.

Sarah exhaled an exasperated breath and wiped her forehead with her arm, but she was beaming. "It was wonderful! We saw so many different animals. You should have come with us."

Wesley was twirling his pen, which caught Sarah's attention. As she focused more on Wesley, she thought he appeared nervous. His eyes darted back and forth, which she had never seen Wesley do. He had always been the personification of calm. "Are you ok?"

"What? … Oh, yes," replied Wesley in a high-pitched voice. Uh … I know this is short notice, but I … uh … I need to go back home. I plan on leaving tomorrow. I must get this article submitted."

Sarah narrowed her eyes, as if getting a better look at this new version of Wesley would identify what was causing his anxiety. She raised her arms, elbows bent and palms facing up. "Can't you just send it in?"

"Reception is really spotty here."

Sarah was about to respond that he had sent information to her at the camp, and she had seen him email his editor. Just as her mouth opened, Wesley interjected. "Besides, the magazine only paid for a few days. If I stay any longer, the cost will come out of my pocket."

Sarah's brow furrowed as she scrunched up her nose. "I'm confused. I thought you paid for this yourself because you were concerned about me … that you wanted to see me."

Wesley emitted a nervous sigh that was almost like a laugh, which was accompanied by a forced and fleeting smile. "Of course, I wanted to see you."

Sarah still wore the confused expression on her face.

Jack walked up, saw Sarah and Wesley talking, and quickly darted beside of a tent. He was out of their line of sight but was in earshot of the conversation. Jack's stomach had a gnawing feeling, and he felt guilty for eavesdropping. Yet, he felt an overwhelming urge to stay and listen.

"Why would the magazine pay for you to come here to see me? That doesn't make any sense.

Wesley ignored the question. "I've been thinking," he replied instead.

"About what?" queried Sarah.

"I think it's time we took the next step. I would like for us to get married. You can work on your Ph.D., and then you can find a job you like that's not in a museum."

Sarah was slow to answer. Jack wanted to peer around the tent to see her expression but didn't dare for fear of being caught.

"I don't know what to say."

"Just think about it."

Jack took a step closer and stepped on a twig, which made a cracking noise as it broke. Had they heard the noise? He didn't want to look to see. Both Sarah and Wesley were quiet. Had the sound caught their attention? He didn't hear footsteps, but he wouldn't unless they were walking on leaves, and Jack was pretty sure the ground was bare. He didn't know how he had the unfortunate luck to step on something. Competing thoughts dashed through his mind. He either needed to turn and leave or walk up as if he were just coming around the corner. As he was debating which to do, he heard Wesley's voice, still at the same distance away. Whether or not they had noticed the sound, they weren't coming his way. Jack focused again on listening and keeping his body still.

"I have an idea for another article." Wesley spoke softer, but Jack could still make out what he was saying.

"It's about the camp, and I think it will be really good. I pitched the idea to the magazine. I could write about how the camp capitalizes on colonialism and the guests' fantasies to relive that bygone era, and the damage it continues to inflict on the indigenous culture."

Jack boiled with such anger that he grew light-headed. He was feeling physically overheated but wanted to go out and punch Wesley. It would feel good in the moment, but he knew that would ultimately do no good and would probably make matters worse. Jack knew he needed to calm down. He noticed that his fists were balled, and his teeth were clinched tightly together. He did his best to relax his body and took a deep breath. He knew he needed to walk away before he heard more, while he had somewhat calmed. Otherwise, he might not be able to control his actions. Jack turned and walked quickly away, heading to find Jill.

🐘 🐘 🐘

Sarah was dumbfounded. For one thing, Wesley's trip to see her was apparently a ruse just to get a story. That would be the only way the magazine would pay for his trip. Did an article mean more to him than she did? And why was Wesley contemplating marriage all of a sudden? He had been quite content with the way their relationship was. What concerned her most though was this article that Wesley mentioned. That would ruin Jack and hurt him emotionally. She had to convince Wesley not to write this article. Would that be possible now since the magazine had paid for the trip? Wesley was also stubborn and selfish when it came to his writing and reporting, but she wouldn't go down without a fight. Seeing Jack ruined because of her, when he had helped so much, would tear her heart out. Plus, no matter how hard she tried to deny it, she had feelings for Jack, and she didn't want to see any harm come to him. "You can't do that. That's not at all what this camp is about. You haven't even done the research to support your claims. That article will end up putting this camp out of business."

Wesley appeared unmoved by Sarah's response. "From what you've told me, the camp is living on borrowed time anyway. This kind of article will sell, and it will give me the exposure I need to finally land the job I want."

"I can't believe you would do such a thing!"

Sarah almost shuttered as Wesley's hands moved down both of her arms, apparently to show her that he was trying to comfort her and calm her down. "It will be good for both of us," assured Wesley. "This camp is on the decline anyway. So what if the article puts it out of business a few months before it would go out of business anyway? We can at least use it for our benefit."

Sarah could hardly believe her ears. She had never heard such rationalizing before for one's own motives, and to hear this from Wesley was even more disturbing. "Who's capitalizing now? You're not the person I thought I knew at all."

The last statement seemed to get Wesley's attention. He looked shocked at what she'd said. His eyes opened so wide they almost bulged, and his mouth hung open like a fish mounted on a wall. He took a deep breath, sighed, and returned to his normal look. "If you're that dead set on me not doing the article, I won't. The main thing is that I want to be with you, and I want you to have stability and a job you like doing. Come back with me. Your vacation time is about over anyway."

Just when Sarah thought Wesley was selfish and didn't care about her, he would surprise her with a comment to the contrary. It had happened before. He sounded sincere. He must be if he was willing to give up on writing the article, she thought. But it also wouldn't surprise her if he wrote the article anyway. She just didn't know if she could trust him. "I can't tomorrow, but I'll go back within a few days."

Wesley nodded, turned, and walked to his tent.

🐘 🐘 🐘

Jill jolted from her chair as the door slammed against the wall. Her heart was pounding, and her hand was clutching her chest as if that would keep her heart from exploding out of her body. She had been absorbed in doing paperwork in the office in the staff lodge when the noise startled her. If there had been any glass panes in the door, the glass would surely have been shattered into hundreds of pieces. When she looked to see what caused the noise, she saw Jack, red-faced, fuming, and snorting like a bull. She was just telling her heart that everything was ok when Jack slammed the door shut. Her heart skipped another beat, and her whole body felt tingly. She closed her eyes and took a deep breath, breathing with her abdomen and letting the air empty her lungs before repeating the process two more times. The whole time, Jack never said a word. When Jill had completely gotten over her fright, she waited for Jack to speak, but he remained silent. She assumed Jack was just begging her to ask; so, she finally did. "You know. For someone who is not saying anything, your thoughts are screaming loudly. What's up?"

Jack was surprisingly much calmer than she expected when he spoke. "I overheard Sarah and Wesley talking. He's going to write an article that will ruin us?"

"What?" Jill could hardly believe she was hearing Jack correctly.

"Yeah. He's going to write how we perpetuate colonialism and anything else to paint us in a negative light. Sarah was probably sent here to do research for him and give him information to use in his article."

To Jill, what Jack had just said sounded like garbled nonsense. She tried to stay calm herself so that Jack wouldn't get worked up any more than he was. "Well, I don't believe Sarah is capable of that. She's had a great time here. Nothing she's done indicates that she feels that way. Now, Wesley … I could see him doing that, but that doesn't mean Sarah has anything to do with it."

Jack paced back and forth in the confined space, the wooden floor creaking with each step. Jill initially followed him with her head, but stopped after a few back and forths; instead, she stared at the dead center of his path. Hopefully, he would look at her when he got to this point.

"It's too much of a coincidence for her not to be in league with him."

"So, she's guilty by association?"

"That pretty much sums it up," Jack replied as he crossed Jill's line of sight.

Jill shook her head and let out an *uh* sound. "You're talking about the same woman you have feelings for, the same woman you were going to tell how you felt about her."

Jack crossed Jill's line of sight again on his back-and-forth pacing route. This time his eyes were shut, and he was rubbing his eyebrows. Jill thought he must have been part bat to stop and turn with his eyes closed without hitting the wall.

"It's the same pattern I fell into the last time I fell for a camp guest. I guess I never learn."

Jack was going over the top in feeling sorry for himself, but Jill felt bad for him and decided not to call him on it. "It's not the same thing at all, and you know it! You had a bad experience with one guest, and you think they are all the same." Hopefully, Jack would see reason and quit expressing universalisms.

"I should have never let myself fall for her."

Jill had to bite her tongue to keep herself from laughing out loud. "If you can control who you are attracted to that well, you need to write a book for the rest of us!"

Jack stopped pacing and looked directly at Jill. "You don't get it. Our business will be ruined as soon as the article is published. We're barely hanging on now."

Jill's face turned red. She did get it. This was what their arguments had been about for the past while. How could he say she didn't get it? "According to you, we are going out of business anyway," she snapped. "What does it matter then if it's next week or next year?"

Jack sat down from his pacing, leaned forward with his head down and put his elbows on his knees. With his hands covering his face, he mumbled, "I just thought she was different." He sat up straight and heaved a heavy sigh.

"I think she is. You just need to give her the chance to show you. Go talk to her."

"I can't face her right now."

"Well, you can hardly avoid her while she's here."

"She'll be leaving soon," Jack said matter-of-factly.

"What are you going to do?"

"We need to get some more supplies anyway. I was going to send Gacoki, but I'll go myself. I'll be back in a few days, and she'll be gone by then."

"So, you're running away?"

"Don't judge me. I just need to get away for a while."

"I think you're making a mistake, but you're a grown man who must make his own decisions. When are you leaving?"

Jack sprang from the chair. "Immediately. Tell Gacoki that he doesn't have to go." He walked with purpose and headed to the door.

"Don't slam the door this time. My heart and nerves can't take any more." Once Jack left, Jill shook her head and mumbled under her breath, "You're making a big mistake."

🐘 🐘 🐘

Sarah knocked on the door to the staff lodge and opened it. Jill looked up from some paperwork she was examining.

"Come in," Jill remarked flatly.

Sarah walked in at the invitation. Jill usually smiled when she saw her, but she showed very little facial expression. Perhaps the paperwork has stressed her, thought Sarah. "Hi, Jill. Have you seen Jack? I really need to tell him something. It's really important."

"I'm afraid he's gone. He left about thirty minutes ago. He overheard Wesley telling you about an article he's going to write that will put us in a very negative light." Jill looked directly into Sarah's eyes. "Is that true?"

That explained Jill's coolness toward her. She couldn't blame her either. Sarah felt guilty even though Wesley was the one who mentioned writing the article. She hoped she could assuage Jill's concerns, and Jack's. "Did Jack hear me try to stop Wesley?"

"I think he left before he heard that part," Jill stated flatly.

She doesn't believe me, thought Sarah. "Jack must think very poorly of me. I didn't ask Wesley to come here. Well, I did ask him to come with me before I left, but Wesley said he was too busy. I certainly didn't want him to come here after ..."

"After you fell for my brother?" interjected Jill.

"Is it that obvious?"

Jill relaxed her body. Sarah had not noticed how tense Jill was until that moment. "It is to everyone but you and Jack. You know that Jack has feelings for you too. He was going to tell you, but then Wesley arrived at the exact moment he was going to tell you. Then, he decided not to say anything. He thought you two were still in love. I hope you're not offended when I say this, but you and Wesley just don't fit. Both of you seem comfortable with the other, but you both are just going through the motions of a relationship; it's not real."

What Jill said resonated with Sarah, perhaps for the first time. It was true; she just hadn't clearly seen it herself. Sarah sighed and plopped down in a chair with her legs spread and her arms by her side as if she were exhausted. Perhaps she was exhausted from all the conflicting feelings that had gone through her head. At the moment, things seemed clear. She loved Jack, not Wesley. "I thought I loved Wesley," Sarah began slowly, "but when I started getting to know Jack, I began to question how I felt about Wesley. I think the relationship I have with Wesley is one of convenience."

"You know. The parallel between you and Amelia is uncanny."

"Gacoki said something similar. But what do you mean? I'm nothing like Amelia."

Jill looked to a corner of the ceiling, as if analyzing Sarah's comment. "You have the stability she had, but your gut tells you that you care for someone else, just like Amelia's gut did."

"I'm so confused, but I need to get back to the museum since my vacation is coming to an end, and I also need to convince Wesley there is a better story to write."

"How do you plan to convince him there is a better story to write?"

"By finding out the ending to what happened with Gordon and Amelia. I know there is something there that we're still missing something that will be a much better story than what Wesley is planning. Weren't there still a few boxes left in the basement that we still haven't gone through?"

"Yes. But only a few. The probability is pretty low that you would find something else. I think the remaining boxes are just old paperwork that probably needs to be thrown out."

"I've got to at least try. Do you mind if I go to the basement and look through the remaining boxes?"

"Not at all. I hope you don't mind doing it by yourself. I really need to finish what I'm doing here."

"I don't mind at all."

"Before you go, what about Jack? Are you going to tell him how you feel about him?"

"How can I if he is not here? Would he even believe me? I think I'm going to have to show him how I feel about him." Sarah started to head to the basement but stopped. "I'm sorry about what all has happened. I feel like everything is my fault."

"Hey. I'm happy to listen. I think you and Jack are good for each other, and I'll do what I can to smooth things over."

"Thank you. I think I'm going to be the only one who can smooth things with Jack."

"If it helps to hear me say it," reassured Jill, "none of this is your fault. I don't know what the future will bring, but we need to have faith that everything will turn out for the best."

Sarah forced a smile to at least appear that she believed Jill regarding her role in all of this. Then, she headed for the basement. Just a day or two ago, Sarah wanted to find out more, but if she didn't, she was satisfied with the information she had discovered about Gordon and Amelia. Now, the ending might make a difference. She didn't know how yet, but she was more determined than ever to find out the ending to the story. And the cryptic statement from Gacoki's grandfather suggested that there was more yet to uncover.

When Sarah reached the basement, she almost felt at home. She had gotten used to the low light, the stale air, and the dust. She wondered why there was still dust left after all of the stirring around they had done. But it all just seemed to resettle. Sarah stared at the small pile of remaining boxes. They seemed to taunt her. Even though the air was still, she imagined them saying, *you won't find anything here.* Her attempt at faith juxtaposed with Jill's comment about the low probability of finding something, and the two warred within her head.

Sarah had looked through all of the remaining boxes, save one. "Only one box left to go," mumbled Sarah to herself. She perused the contents and then slapped the lid back on. "Jill was right. There's nothing in any of these that is relevant. Everything's basically out-of-date paperwork." Sarah's stomach knotted. She had confidently told Jill that she would find a better story to write, but she had failed. The only thing to hope for now was that Wesley would be true to his word and not write an article if she asked him not to.

She didn't like putting that much faith in Wesley. Looking back over the years as an observer, she could see his self-centeredness. Even concern for her, upon scrutiny, devolved into what was ultimately good for himself. Love, or whatever version of that she had with Wesley, truly was blind.

Sarah walked around the basement, hoping the knot in her stomach would go away. She continued mumbling to herself. "We've been through all of the boxes. I'm afraid I'm at a dead end." She had made several laps around the basement when something sticking out from the bottom corner of a shelving unit caught her eye. It was barely visible and was at the back of the shelving unit against the wall. Dust covered, it blended in with the floor. "What do we have here?" Sarah closed her eyes and said a prayer before walking over to the shelving unit to investigate. She stooped down, grabbed what small tip was exposed, and pulled. It wouldn't budge. It was difficult to move because it was wedged between the shelving unit and the wall. She tugged harder and pushed the shelving unit with her shoulder. She was able to force a little more of the object out. It was a folder. Sarah pushed again with her shoulder and worked the folder side to side while pulling until it finally pulled free. She wiped the dust off the folder, which caused her to cough and sneeze. She closed her eyes and prayed one more time. Then she opened it. A smile formed on her face, which grew wider as she shuffled through the contents of the folder. She clutched the folder to her chest and ran up the stairs.

Jill wasn't upstairs; she had apparently finished whatever paperwork she had been working on. Sarah opened the door to darkness. How long had she been in the basement, she wondered? She looked at her watch and gasped when she noticed the time. She had missed dinner. Of course, she was too excited to be hungry. Where would Jill be? At this hour, Jill would probably be in the social tent. Using the flashlight on her phone, she hurried to the social tent. Walking in, she searched for Jill and finally saw her behind the bar where a few guests were having a drink. She hurried over, still clutching the folder.

"Hey," greeted Jill. "You must have lost track of the time. Dinner is already over, but I can find something for you though."

"I'm too excited to eat anything!" replied Sarah.

Jill gasped, and her eyes grew wide. "Did you find something?"

"Yes. I think it's the last piece of the puzzle." Sarah smiled for so long and her smile was so wide that her cheeks began to ache. Euphoria filled every inch of her body to the point that she was almost shaking. "I saw some photos, a letter, and a newspaper article, but I wanted to wait to read everything with you and Jack. Did he come back?"

Sarah's enthusiasm was contagious and had gotten Jill excited. But the question about Jack caused her to grow suddenly solemn. Jill looked at Sarah with apologetic eyes. "I'm afraid not. It may be a couple of days yet before he gets back."

"I don't think I can't wait any longer. I'm dying to find out what this says. Do you want to look at this with me?"

"Are you kidding? I've been dying to find out more too. Let's go over to the corner."

Even though Jill had indicated otherwise, Sarah was afraid that Jill still harbored ill feelings toward her over Wesley's potential article. To see Jill smiling and excited lifted a tremendous weight from Sarah and made the joy of sharing this new information that much greater.

Sarah and Jill found an empty corner. The buzzing hum of conversations and people playing games wafted their way, but Sarah and Jill could easily hear each other and talk without distracting others. "What should I start with," asked Sarah?

"We've been looking at Amelia's diary." Jill pointed to another leather-bound book. "That looks like another diary. Let's start with that."

Sarah picked up the book. Like before, she rubbed the leather with her hand feeling the graininess of the texture. She opened the precious diary and began to read.

Chapter 18

Anthony could hardly wait until the trucks were completely loaded. Talking with Thomas had been difficult for numerous reasons. First, how do you tell someone that your sister isn't going to marry them after all? Second, the news would be scandalous back home. Anthony and his parents would be social pariahs, especially since Thomas was a future duke. Third, bearing the anger and insults from Thomas was ... well ... insulting. Fourth, he would be accompanying Thomas the entire way back to England. Fifth, he had to endure the continued whispering of Amelia's friends. He was sure that there were more reasons, but dealing with five was plenty to occupy him for the time being. Once he got back home, there would be a whole new set of issues to deal with. Chief among them would be telling his parents, or rather explaining to his parents. No doubt, they would already know by the time his feet touched English soil.

Even with all of this, his main concern was Amelia. He wasn't worried about her and Gordon. He was sure Amelia would have a happy life with Gordon, much better than the life she would have had with Thomas. He dreaded not having Amelia in his life. He had to face the fact that he would rarely, if ever, see her again, at least not for a long time. Letters would have to be their primary means of communication, if letters could even find their way to her. He had already been parted from his sister once before for several years during the Great War. Although Amelia was only a few years younger than him, she had seemed like a little girl when he left for the Great War. She cried and begged him not to leave, which was unusual for Amelia. That was the only time in his life that he remembered seeing Amelia cry. When he returned home four years later, she had grown even more independent. But they picked back up as though he had never left. Anthony had always been a buffer between Amelia and their parents. Being without him for four years and facing their parents on her own had taken a toll on Amelia even though she wouldn't admit it. He didn't want to think about another long separation. They, of course, bantered like brothers and sisters do, but he loved her, and he knew she loved him. Gordon would be the primary man in her life now, but Anthony knew she would miss him.

The sorrow that flooded Anthony as he thought about Amelia immediately dissipated at the sight of Thomas exiting his tent. He was carrying a rifle. Anthony blocked his movement and put a hand out to further halt him. "Whoa. What are you doing with that?"

"Isn't it obvious," scowled Thomas. "I'm going to look for Lady Amelia and that scoundrel."

Even in anger, Thomas wore aristocratic entitlement like a well-cut tuxedo. If Anthony weren't completely unnerved, he would have probably laughed. Thomas was like a gentleman who had been slapped in the face with a glove and was going to seek vengeance through an old-fashioned duel. Rather than dueling pistols though, he had a hunting rifle.

"I told you. They aren't here. Please, put the gun down before someone gets hurt." Anthony grabbed for the gun, but Thomas jerked it away before he could confiscate it.

"Get your hands off me and leave me alone. Besides, I don't believe a word you're saying about those two not being here. You've been in on this from the start. Of all the guides you could choose, you chose your ruffian friend with whom you never should have associated in the first place. You knew this would happen. You deserve to have your title stripped from you, and when we get back to England, I'll make sure that happens. I have the ear of His Majesty, King George V, and when he hears of this, you'll be stripped of everything. You might as well head for America or Australia now." Thomas marched off through a pocket of dense vegetation making an inordinate amount of noise as he crashed through the vegetation.

Anthony debated going after him but decided against it. Thomas wouldn't find Amelia and Gordon, and hopefully, the walk would give him a chance to regain his composure. By then, the trucks would be loaded, and they could make the arduous journey back to England.

About thirty minutes had passed, and Thomas had not returned, but Anthony hadn't expected him to return yet. He figured that Thomas would spend about an hour thrashing about and huffing to give a good show of effort before returning to camp. The last of their belongings was being loaded into the last truck. Amelia's friends were already in the jeep. Due to the heat of sitting in the jeep, Anthony told their driver to head to Nairobi, and Thomas and he would meet them there. About fifteen minutes had passed, and the jeep was out of sight when Anthony heard a gunshot.

Anthony raced through the vegetation, fearing that Amelia and Gordon had indeed returned to the camp. He had heard only one shot, and thoughts of Amelia or Gordon lying dead raced through his mind urging him to move as fast as his legs would take him. He headed in the general direction of the sound of the gunshot, hoping his sense of direction would lead him to the right spot. The first person Anthony saw was Kagiso. Slowly, his mind registered that Kagiso was kneeling over a bloodied body. Kagiso was checking for a pulse. As he closed in, he focused on the body lying on the ground. Anthony's heart was pounding as he crashed awkwardly through the vegetation. His heart was pounding in his ears, and he was gasping for breath. Fear engulfed him. He was light-headed and felt as though he were going to pass out. Part of Anthony's mind questioned why he was so fearful. He had seen people killed. He had killed. He had faced death himself. But that was war. This was his personal life and possibly family. Then, he got a better view of the body. Thank goodness it wasn't Amelia, and a short-lived wave of relief spread through him. But the stench of blood that attacked his nose sent new waves of fear through him. Vaguely, outside of his focus, his mind registered another person standing nearby with a rifle. He focused on the man with the rifle, but confusion clouded his mind. Anthony was suddenly outside of his body, looking at the horrific scene as if he were an ethereal observer. He had heard about certain out-of-body experiences from soldiers severely injured during the war, and he wondered if he, himself, had been shot and was now looking down over his dead body. His heartbeat throbbing in his ears told him that he was alive, and that thought slowly unclouded his mind. He wondered who the person was on the ground. Back and forth, he alternated looks between the man with the rifle and the body on the ground. The man with the rifle wasn't Thomas. He wasn't Gordon. Anthony didn't recognize the man. Then, he looked more closely at the man lying on the ground. Kagiso looked up at Anthony and shook his head. The man on the ground was dead. Nausea enveloped him. The man on the ground was Thomas.

For several seconds, words would not come to Anthony. Vocabulary and the sight of Thomas lying dead would not coexist in his mind. Words finally came to him when he heard the man with the rifle clear his throat.

"What happened? Is he dead?" Anthony already knew the answer to the second question, but he had to hear it said.

"I'm afraid he is dead," answered Kagiso. "I heard a gunshot and ran over to find him on the ground. I suspect some hunters thought he was an animal and shot him. The bullet pierced his jugular vein. He lost a lot of blood and died quickly."

"Did you see anything?" Anthony asked the man with the rifle, who was obviously a hunter.

"I heard a shot and a noise and came over to find these two men just as they are now." The hunter didn't look Anthony in the eyes, and Anthony noticed that the hunter was breathing short, shallow breaths. "I need to report this to the authorities," and he hurried away.

Rationality took control of Anthony's mind, and he quickly assessed the situation and possible outcomes. "The hunter was probably the one who shot Thomas."

Kagiso nodded. "I imagine you are right. The hunter will probably blame me since I was first to arrive."

"I know you didn't shoot Thomas, but others might not believe you. It should be your word against that of the hunter. And both of you have similar rifles. But it will come out that Amelia left Thomas for Gordon. Since you, Gordon, and I are all friends, that will definitely raise suspicion. And it is highly unlikely that the wound was self-inflicted. I hate to suggest this, but it might be best if you leave the area for a while."

"I fear you are right, though leaving will probably cast further suspicion on me. I would rather be a wanted man than falsely imprisoned or sentenced to death."

"The hunter doesn't know who you are, and I can say I'd never seen you before. It won't be long before it is safe for you again."

Anthony didn't like Thomas very much, but he certainly didn't want him dead. Thomas' death would complicate matters even more for his family. He had already thought they couldn't get worse; he should never have thought that. "I'm happy for Amelia and Gordon, but I'm sorry that things are ending the way they are. I hope to see you again, my friend."

Anthony and Kagiso hugged each other. Anthony didn't want to let go. In his heart, he knew this would probably be the last he ever saw of Kagiso, one of the two men who had saved his life. Abruptly, they let go. Anthony headed back to the disassembled camp, and Kagiso went in another direction. Ultimately, Anthony would be right. That was the last time the two men would see each other.

🐘 🐘 🐘

Sarah finished reading the diary entry, and both women were quiet for several seconds.

Jill was the first to speak. "Oh, no. That's awful."

"I know. I wonder what happened to Kagiso."

"Keep reading. Maybe the diary will tell."

Sarah turned the page to the next entry.

🐘 🐘 🐘

Small ripple-like waves lapped against the sugary, white sand of an east Kenyan beach, south of Mombasa. A gentle breeze off the turquoise waters of the Indian Ocean caressed Amelia's face, cooling it from the warm noon sunlight. Amelia rose to a seated position on the blanket, wrapping her arms around her knees, just in time to see the graceful arch of a dolphin. Behind a row of coconut palm trees stood their simple hut. Birds chirped cheerful songs, and the smell of mangoes scented the air. She looked to make sure Gordon was beside her. She knew he was, but she could never get enough of seeing him. Amelia rubbed her hand through the thick, chestnut brown hair on Gordon's chest, waking him. A contented sigh escaped her lips. "May we stay here forever?"

"Fine by me. We own the hut. As long as you don't mind eating fish and fruit every day, we never have to leave."

Amelia's eyes twinkled, and she spoke in her sensual, smoky-velvet voice that drove Gordon wild with passion. "What about my gin and your bourbon?"

Gordon opened his eyes and sat up, matching Amelia's pose like two bookends. "I have some money saved up. We can use it on gin and bourbon." Adding a smile, "I've seen money wasted on worse things."

"I wonder what kind of alcohol one could make from coconuts?" Amelia asked, furrowing her brow. "Maybe you could fly one of those moonshiners you spoke about from the States, and they could set up a still and teach us how to make our own."

Amelia snuggled up to Gordon and laid her head on his shoulder. "Are you thinking about Kagiso?"

Gordon sighed. "Yes. You must be a mind reader. I hope he is ok. I think things will eventually blow over concerning Thomas' death. Now that we're married, I wonder what Kagiso will do. He has his own life to live, but I was used to seeing him every day."

"Kagiso watched over you to make sure no harm came to you."

"You mean to make sure I didn't harm myself or keep me from doing something stupid to bring me harm?"

"I don't know how successful he was at that. I mean you are known for going after man-eating cats. He didn't stop you from doing that."

"You are right about the fact that he watched over me."

"Am I supposed to take care of you now? I didn't know I signed up for that duty when I married you."

"It was in the fine print when you signed the marriage license. Did you not notice it? Besides, I think it has been the other way around. I've had to watch over you to keep you from doing stupid things like going out by yourself to pee in the middle of the night when I told you not to!"

"Apparently, you haven't been too successful either."

"Apparently. I had to marry you to keep a closer watch on you."

"That was my plan. Rather ingenious, don't you think?"

"You drive me crazy when you talk in that voice. Don't ever stop. Was that part of the plan too?"

"Ah, you've got the goods on me. Isn't that what you Americans say?"

"This American says, I love you. I know you gave up a lot to marry me."

"Stop right there. I gained a lot by marrying you. And you didn't do too badly yourself!"

"I can see you are going to be a handful, Mrs. Powell."

"Not too much of a handful, I hope. I'd like to keep my figure for a while at least until we start having babies." Amelia looked out over the ocean, closed her eyes, and deeply inhaled a scent of mangoes mixed with salty air. She dug her feet into the fine, white sand, stuck out her toes and wiggled them, watching the sand fall off. "You know. "This place is nearly perfect. Once we have children running around, they will spoil everything. I think when the time comes, we'll have to move back inland and leave this spot untainted."

"I know you're kidding."

"Of course, I am."

"You're saying that because you think I'll go crazy if we don't eventually go back to the savanna, but you're wrong. I could stay here with you for the rest of my life."

"I know you could, but I think eventually we should go back. We still need to keep our place here though. In case all of those kids start driving us crazy, we'll have a place to run off to."

"Deal."

Amelia leaned in and kissed Gordon. Her blonde locks caressed his face. They stood up, left their blanket on the beach, and walked, hand in hand, to their hut.

🐘 🐘 🐘

Satisfaction filled Sarah as she finished the last sentence. For however long they lived, at least they were happy in the moment. That was what Sarah was hoping for Gordon ever since she saw the photo in the Colorado museum of the man with the sad eyes. That look had struck her to her core and had been the impetus for this incredible journey of discovery, both for Sarah and for the story of Gordon Powell. Connection, as Amelia had told Gordon, was key to him winning his hellish battle against the damage the Great War had inflicted on him. She had also come to terms with her grandfather's battle with PTSD. He found moments of connection with his wife, with Sarah, and with the Powell Camp. He may not have found an ever-present connection, but he loved and was loved. In the end, that's all that anyone could ask for. If not for her curiosity, the last chapter of the story of Gordon Powell could have closed with the diary entry that Sarah had just finished reading. But she wanted more of the story, even though she knew it might not have the tidy ending she just read.

Sarah was in her own world, oblivious to Jill's voice. Eventually, the recesses of her mind heard a question that might have been asked several times.

"What's next?" begged Jill.

This seemed to be Jill's favorite question, one that she consistently asked, thought Sarah. Her curiosity seemed as strong as Sarah's. The reason for her curiosity was perhaps different. Ultimately, both women's curiosity boiled down to family. Jill, being orphaned in her early teens, probably wanted to learn all she could about her ancestor while Sarah's curiosity had much to do with learning more about her grandfather's battle for emotional freedom.

Sarah quickly flipped through the diary. "There's not much more after this, just a few disjointed statements. It's definitely not the same writing style as before. The entries look more like notes than diary narrative. She says that after two years on the coast, she and Gordon moved back and started this camp using money she inherited that Anthony sent her when their father died. Gordon was really adamant about protecting the wildlife; so, he led people on sightseeing safaris, much like you do now. They had some famous people as part of their clientele. She has a list of names, which she apparently wrote down after the fact." Sarah turned a few more pages, which were blank. "Here's another page with writing. It looks like a list of ideas for the camp. "Amelia wrote that they and the camp fell on some hard times during World War II, and the Italian army penetrated into the northern part of Kenya. Although that was still far from the camp, the camp was closed for several years. She listed some ideas to help the camp bounce back after the war, but they never acted on them. Most of these sound almost identical to what you and Gacoki want to do. I haven't seen anything else yet about Kagiso." Sarah turned to the next page. "This is interesting. She turned the diary so that both she and Jill could see what was written. "Look at what she wrote."

Dear Diary,

Sorry I haven't written much in such a long time. In fact, this will be the last entry I plan on writing. You allowed me to express what I couldn't tell others, that is, until I married Gordon and until Anthony and I started sharing correspondence. Why am I neglecting you, you ask? Well, the reason is quite simple. I no longer need a diary as a way to cope with the stifled life I led previously. I live in the moment, and it's truly a wonderful way to live. I'm sorry to have taken advantage of you. Please forgive me.

Yours truly,

Amelia Powell

"She writes to her diary as if it's a person," exclaimed Jill. "It is inspiring though."

Sarah flipped through the remaining pages. "That's all there is."

"I wonder if they ever saw Kagiso again? What's left in the folder?"

Sarah looked through the folder and pulled out an envelope that had been opened neatly with a letter opener. She pulled the letter out, unfolded it, and examined it for several seconds. "This is a letter from the executor of her brother's will." She read some more and then summarized the content for Jill. "Apparently, at some point, Anthony married. It seems that Anthony and his wife were killed during the bombings of London in World War II. They had a daughter, and they left most everything they had to her. The peerage Anthony held could only pass to the next male in the line of succession; so, Anthony's peerage ended with him. He left some of his wealth to Amelia; he felt that their father didn't leave enough to Amelia, and he wanted to make up for that. But, as I said, most of what he had went to his daughter."

Jill sighed. "That's heartbreaking. It's sad that Anthony survived the fighting in World War I as a soldier but was killed as a civilian in World War II due to the bombings of London." Jill looked to be deep in thought. "I wonder why nothing was mentioned about Anthony getting married in Amelia's diary?"

"I don't know. He must have married after Amelia stopped writing as much in her diaries. Her diary did say that she and Anthony had lots of correspondence. It's too bad we don't have any of that correspondence. Surely, Amelia would have kept it, but it must not have been saved with her diaries. I would love to have those letters."

"We're fortunate to have found what we did. That's a miracle in itself after all this time."

"The only things left in the folder appear to be various photos of Gordon and Amelia, the camp, a child who I suppose was their son, and some of the people whom Gordon led on safaris. Wow!" Sarah's jaw dropped and her eyes widened. "I recognize some of these guests as famous people, politicians, heads of state, celebrities." Sarah paused. "Wait! Here's a letter stuck between two photos, and there's an envelope at the very bottom of the box."

"Well, hurry up and read them!"

"The one stuck between the photos is a letter dated from 1960 from Amelia." Sarah began reading.

Dear Gordon,

The doctors say that I don't have much time left; so, I thought I would write to you like you wrote to your brother, Grant, after he was killed. I'll see you soon, and the first thing I want to do is hold you and kiss you with my wild, golden curls brushing against your face. So, I want to get some of your questions answered first so that they do not interrupt our first meeting in the afterlife. Our son is doing well and will pick up running the camp. I finally saw Kagiso. He showed up out of the blue to pay his respects. He said he was very sorry that he missed your funeral. He was also very sad when I told him that Anthony had been killed during the bombings of London in World War 2. He told me how he grieved when he left Anthony after Thomas' death. He said he knew then that would be the last time he would ever see Anthony. Kagiso said that the three of you surviving the Battle of the Selle was a miracle and that all of you were living on borrowed time. He just wished that you and Anthony had as much time as he had. I hope you don't mind, but I gave him your dog tag. As you know, we buried Grant's dog tag with you so that you could give it to him when you saw him. I couldn't part with yours. But seeing as I don't have much time left, I wanted to give it to someone who still remembered that horrible war and the friendship that came from it. I've also willed that our beach hut and property on the coast be given to the camp. Well, that's all the news I have. I'll see you soon.

Your forever love,

Amelia

Sarah looked at Jill when she finished the letter. Jill had a confounded look on her face – glazed eyes, head tilted slightly down, and her chin resting between thumb and forefinger. Sarah playfully snapped her fingers in front of Jill's eyes. Jill blinked and came out of her temporary paralysis.

"I'm sorry," apologized Jill. "I was thinking about one of the sentences in the letter. I don't know anything about the camp owning property on the coast. I'll need to check with an attorney. It's doubtful that it would still belong to us after all of these years."

Sarah was in a confounded state herself, which she snapped out of when Jill returned the favor of snapping her fingers in front of Sarah's eyes.

"Did you hear anything I said?" inquired Jill.

"I'm sorry. A line in the letter caught my attention as well. I think I may have seen Gordon's dog tab."

Jill's eyes grew wide. "Really? Where?"

"Gacoki's grandfather had two dog tags that he wore around his neck. When I asked him about Gordon and Kagiso, he said to come back when I had specific questions to ask. Well, I do have some specific questions to ask him now." A sense of urgency entered Sarah's voice. "I have to go see him!"

"It's too late and dangerous to go now. You'll need to wait until the morning. I'll ask Gacoki to take you. Don't forget about the last letter in the box," piped Jill.

"Oh … thanks for reminding me. I had forgotten about it after remembering about the dog tags." Sarah picked up the envelope. It was lopsided and apparently held an object inside. Sarah looked at

Jill and smiled, eager to see what the last object in the box was, hopefully one of the final pieces of the puzzle. She looked at the outside of the envelope, and shock spread across her face draining her color as it spread. Sarah's mouth dropped open.

Jill looked over with a concerned expression on her face. "Is something the matter?"

"I don't understand." She handed the envelope to Jill, who appeared confused.

Jill observed the letter. "It has a postmark dated much later than what we've been seeing. It must have been placed in the box by mistake." Jill looked at the letter again. I don't know any Robert Jacobs, and this is addressed to my father." Jill paused suddenly, "Jacobs. That's the same as your last name. Robert Jacobs was my grandfather's name."

Jill looked over. She had one eyebrow raised in an arch while the other remained level. Jill simultaneously said, "What?" while opening the letter. She scanned the letter, repeating, "Oh, My," several times.

"I wonder if it is really my grandfather or some other Robert Jacobs."

"I'm pretty sure it's your grandfather. It's typewritten but it has a signature at the bottom. Do you recognize this as your grandfather's?" Jill turned the letter so that Sarah could see it.

"It's been a long time, and I'm not completely sure, but I think so. You read it; I don't think I can."

Jill began to read.

Dear Mr. Powell,

I enjoyed my trip to Africa and to your camp. It was one of the best times of my life, and I hope to make another trip if I can. I'm glad you took my advice and reached out to the U.S Army Awards and Decorations Branch. I know there were some hoops to jump through, but I'm glad you were able to get the Purple Heart posthumously awarded to Gordon Powell. Having the newspaper articles certainly helped in documenting his injuries. A man of his bravery certainly deserved it. Although I never met Gordon Powell, I certainly connected with him. Being a Vietnam Veteran and a Purple Heart recipient myself, I think I have some understanding of what he went through. Each war has its own horrors. Sometimes the memories are overwhelming. I appreciate your letter letting me know you received it. I look forward to hopefully seeing you and your father again.

Sincerely,

Robert Jacobs

"Our families were already connected," bubbled Jill. She looked over to see tears streaming down Sarah's face. Hugging Sarah tightly, she added, "I think you were meant to see this to help put your mind at ease with your grandfather."

"It's almost like Gordon, Amelia, and my grandfather were in heaven concocting this whole adventure to tell their stories to us."

"I can believe that," answered Jill in a soothing voice.

"I'm so glad I came here to find out about Gordon Powell. It has been very therapeutic for me. Not only have I questioned my happiness with my job, but it has helped me mentally to close a chapter on my emotional turmoil with my grandfather's inner war. Before coming here, I don't think I could have imagined having this much peace with it."

Chapter 19

The next morning, the trip to the village seemed to take no time at all. Sarah was engrossed in thought about what she planned to ask and about the potential answers. She didn't remember being jolted by the jeep or hitting any potholes. One minute she was at the camp, and seemingly, in the blink of an eye, she was at the village, standing in front of the hut of Gacoki's grandfather.

Gacoki knocked on the door. "Grandfather." Shortly, Gacoki's grandfather opened the door and smiled when he saw Sarah.

"Where's Jack?" he asked. "I thought you two would be together by now."

A sheepish look came over Sarah's face. "He's a little mad at me at the moment, but I plan on remedying that."

Gacoki's grandfather chuckled. "A strong fire always requires a little friction to get started." He motioned for Gacoki and Sarah to come inside. "I was wondering when you would be back. I was starting to give up hope."

"Information about Gordon Powell has been hard to come by."

"Apparently, you found some. I assume you have some specific questions now that you want to ask?"

"Yes. The first question burst from Sarah's mouth. "Are the dog tags you're wearing Gordon's and Kagiso's?"

The grandfather smiled. Sarah thought that he had a distant look in his eyes as he caressed the two identification tags between his thumb and forefinger. "They are," he replied after a slight pause. Kagiso was my father. I am Kagiso's only child and was born when he was much older. He lived to a ripe old age and would tell me stories about Gordon Powell and him. I'll tell you some of them, if you have time."

"I have plenty of time." Sarah looked to Gacoki to see if that was alright with him since he was the one who drove.

"But first, I'll answer your questions," continued the grandfather. "Gordon was one of my father's true friends, probably because of the horrors they shared in the Great War."

"Why did they not see each other after Gordon married Amelia? Surely after a while no one would have questioned Kagiso about Thomas' death."

"Probably not. Supposedly, Anthony told the police that he didn't know who the man was who found Thomas. What my father said was that once Gordon married Amelia, he knew that Gordon would be alright. He intended to see him, but time passes before we realize it. World War II didn't help matters. Due to his marksmanship and service in World War I, Kagiso helped train soldiers for the King's African Rifles." He paused, in apparent introspection. "The seasons of life pass quickly. In the summer of one's life, a person comes to fullness and lives as they choose, thinking they will remain that way forever. Before they realize it, twenty years have slipped away, and they are in the autumn of life and thinking about the winter, wondering how it all happened so quickly. Gordon told my father about an American named Benjamin Franklin who said something like, *Life's tragedy is that we get old too soon and wise too late.* I guess I said all of that to say that Kagiso had intended to see Gordon again, but then it was too late."

"Thank you for telling me."

"Now, how about some of those stories I promised."

"I would love to hear them."

Chapter 20

The next day, Sarah, Jill, and Gacoki stood next to a jeep. Sarah had waited as long as possible before leaving. She wouldn't have much time to spare to make it back to Nairobi and her flight back to the States. Although she knew she could change her flight, she wanted to get back to find out if Wesley planned on writing an article about the camp after all. Plus, Sean hadn't approved any additional time off. "So, Jack still hasn't come back yet?"

"No," answered Jill. "Do you have to leave now? Can you wait a little longer?"

"I wish I could, but I need to give this story to Wesley and make sure he isn't writing what he originally planned."

"Goodbye." Jill's eyes were moist with tears. "We are all going to miss you."

"I will miss all of you too. Tell Jack ... well, never mind."

"Your car is filled with petrol, and your tires are fine, including the spare," grinned Gacoki.

Sarah got into her rental car and waved as she drove off.

The flights back to Colorado were long and tiring. Once she made it home, she called Wesley and asked to meet him at their favorite restaurant. She rehearsed in her head what she planned to say, but finally decided to just go with what her heart said in the moment. Sarah arrived at the restaurant earlier than Wesley and was sitting at a table when he entered. He spotted her right away and made his way to the table. Sarah stood, and she and Wesley hugged each other and sat down.

"Thanks for meeting me, Wesley."

"Of course. I don't know about you, but I couldn't wait to get some familiar food when I left Kenya. This was the first place I came to when I got back. I didn't even go home first! I have to tell you; my bill was pretty expensive by the time I left."

"I enjoyed the food I had in Kenya, but I do love this restaurant."

"I know I can be inattentive at times, but when you called, I sensed a purpose and urgency in your voice. What's up?"

"Are you still planning on writing the article about Powel's African Camp and Safari?" Sarah had blurted the question out and hoped it didn't come across as rude or even worse, desperate.

Wesley looked up from the menu in his hands. "I told you that if you didn't want me to write it, I wouldn't. I haven't written anything."

"I want you to read this. I made photocopies of Amelia's diaries and notes I took." Sarah held out the folder with all of the materials.

Wesley looked puzzled. "Why are you giving me this?"

"You said that to get the job you wanted, you needed to go beyond facts and to show something from the heart. I think you'll find it in here."

"Wait. I'm confused. So, now you want me to write the article?"

"Well, not the original article you planned to write. I hope you will write something positive and heartfelt."

Wesley took the folder. "I'll look through it. If I can't find something positive to write, then I won't write anything." He looked into Sarah's eyes. "I promise." After he put the folder in his briefcase, he hesitated and looked down at the table.

Sarah knew what was coming next and hoped she was prepared to answer honestly.

"What did you decide ... about us and your life?"

"I do love you, but I can't marry you." There. She said it, and saying it wasn't as difficult as she thought it would be. The words of Gacoki's grandfather about the passage of time entered her mind, and she knew her decision was the right one.

"Is it Jack?" Wesley averted his eyes as he asked the question.

Sarah knew this would be a difficult conversation for him. "Partly, but it's also me. It's true that I have stability here, but life is about more than stability. I learned that by reading Amelia's diary.

I'm really sorry."

"Don't be sorry to do something you want. That was one of the admirable characteristics of Amelia, a true strength. She went for what she wanted. Are you certain this is what you want? After a while, you might feel as stuck as you did at the museum."

"I don't think so. I feel at peace there, and there is a lot of research I can do."

"Well, I hope we both get what we want."

Sarah reached across the table and laid her hand atop Wesley's hand. "I hope so too. One of my most heartfelt wishes is that you are happy."

Wesley smiled. "Since we're here, we might as well eat, and I'll buy. I hope we can do that as friends."

"Of course. I'm famished, but I'll try not to go overboard, especially since you said you were buying." Both Sarah and Wesley chuckled.

"Order whatever you want. We do have some toasting to do, and for that we need a good bottle of wine."

Sarah awoke earlier than she expected the next morning. Apparently, jetlag had not yet hit her. Today's main goal was to go to the museum to talk with Sean. A small bit of guilt settled within her. Letting Sean know that she was resigning might put him on the spot. The Board was expecting to showcase the museum's new direction on a specific date. Leaving Sean shorthanded wasn't a pleasant thought, but she would put in a two-week notice. Sean probably wouldn't be able to fill the position by then, but she could work extra. She didn't want to work more than two weeks because she didn't want to let much more time go by without trying to patch things up with Jack.

The small display of Gordon Powell in the museum came to the forefront of her mind. The trip to Kenya had been partly to find some convincing evidence to keep it. Her resignation would probably hurt what little chance there was of convincing Sean to keep it. But whatever the decision, she would be ok with it.

On the way to work, Sarah stopped to get a cup of coffee. Although drinking coffee hadn't been a normal part of her daily routine, except for an occasional Starbuck's coffee prior to traveling to Kenya, she had developed a taste for it while there. Unfortunately, the coffee was not nearly as good as what she had in Kenya.

She arrived early at work to find that Sean's car was already there. When she entered the museum, she barely recognized it. The museum was littered with new pieces that needed writeups, and decisions would have to be made as to where to put them. Fortunately, she wouldn't be the one deciding where they went, but writing up descriptions would be her job. Getting to Sean's office was like traveling through a maze. She hit more than one dead end before finding her way to Sean's office. Traversing the course reminded her of a mouse hunting for a piece of cheese in a maze. When she entered his office, Sean was standing in the middle of it. He seemed frazzled. His hair was standing on end, and his clothes were disheveled looking.

"I'm glad you're back," he said when he saw her. Then, he began pacing back and forth. "We really have a lot of work to do." He paused as if he had forgotten something. "Oh, how was your vacation? I hope you had a good time and found what you were looking for."

"About that."

"Sarah, let's not get into this conversation again about keeping the Powell exhibit. I need you to be focused if we're going to have our grand reopening on time."

"I really need to tell you something."

"Can't it wait? As you can see, we have quite a mess here at the moment."

"I'm resigning." She hadn't meant to blurt it out like that, but she couldn't seem to get Sean's attention otherwise.

Sean stopped dead in his tracks from pacing at hearing the pronouncement. His face drained of color, turning white as a sheet. She hoped he wouldn't pass out. Immediately, Sarah went to the water cooler in Sean's office and filled a cup with water. She took it to him and placed it in his hand. "Here. Drink this. You look as though you might pass out."

"Tell me you didn't just say what I thought you said." Sean looked for a place to sit, and Sarah rolled his chair over to where he was standing.

"Sit for a minute. I don't like the looks of you right now."

"Gee! Thanks for the compliment." At least he had a little sense of humor, she thought. "You can't leave now! There's so much work to be done."

"I'll work the mandatory two weeks."

"It's going to take more than two weeks to put all of this together, and I'll never find anyone to take your place on such short notice. Is this about the Powell exhibit? Would you really quit your job over it?"

"I am sort of quitting because of it but not in the way you think. I totally understand that it doesn't fit the new direction."

"I'm afraid I don't understand. You're quitting because of it but not because of it. That doesn't make any sense."

Sarah briefly explained her trip to Kenya and what she found out, explaining only the relevant parts. However, she did tell Sean she had fallen in love with Gordon's descendant, Jack, and how her job at the museum wasn't what she wanted any longer.

"That's quite an interesting story. And you say your boyfriend … er … ex-boyfriend, Wesley, is going to write an article about it?"

"He may write an article about it. I hope he does. It will make for a good story, and if he writes it the way I hope, it might help his career as well."

"Ok. I give up. We'll keep it, but it will have to go in a corner somewhere. We can probably come up with some rationale for keeping it."

"I'm still leaving after two weeks."

"I understand, and I wasn't trying to use it as a bargaining chip to get you to stay. The offer is unconditional. But you'll have to write up something new for it, and it will have to be on your own time."

"Thank you, Sean. Listen. I'll put in overtime to help the museum get ready for its grand reopening, and you don't have to pay extra for it."

"Well, I don't think Human Resources would approve, but I'm going to take you up on that offer. What Human Resources doesn't know won't hurt them."

Sarah laughed followed by Sean's laughter.

"Now, get to work!"

"Yes sir."

The first week went by quickly. Sarah was in by six o'clock every morning and worked until midnight every night, and she worked through lunch, except for one day. That day, she called a friend who was a professor at the University of Colorado Boulder in the cultural anthropology graduate program. The professor knew of a graduate of the program who lived nearby and was looking for a job. Sean hired her on a temporary basis, telling her that if she worked out ok, she could have Sarah's job. Between Sarah and the temp, the museum work was ahead of schedule. Jetlag never set in, and the anticipation of getting back to Kenya kept her going. She seemed to have a boundless supply of energy.

Exactly one week after arriving back in Colorado, Wesley called. Excitement filled his voice, and Sarah thought she had never heard him that excited about anything ever in his life. "Hey, I wanted to let you know that I finished the article. My editor said it was the best piece I've ever written and that it showed the heart and human element that he wanted me to have in my writing. It's going to be published any day now. I've sent you an advance copy; I think you will really like it."

"That's great news! I'm so happy for you, and I look forward to reading it."

"Thank you for giving me such good material to work with and for encouraging me to do better. There's something else I wanted to ask you."

He paused on the phone, and Sarah wondered if he was gathering the courage to ask. She wondered what he was going to ask and if it would be something she could agree to. "What do you want to ask?"

"Well ... uh ... I was wondering if ... er ... if I could have permission to write a biographical novel of Gordon Powell."

"What?"

"Well, I've always wanted to try my hand at writing a book, and this seems perfect for it."

"How come I never knew that?"

"Probably because I kept it secret. I was so driven to establish myself as a respected journalist that I always kept the idea on the back burner. But I've got the outline in mind, and I think I can do that while also continuing to work as an investigative reporter. Of course,

I wouldn't write anything to implicate Kagiso in Thomas' death. I've thought of a way to work around that." Wesley paused. Sarah knew he was awaiting her response.

"I think that's a great idea. You have my permission. Most of the diary entries belong to Powell's African Camp and Safari; so, I suppose they would have to give their permission as well, but I think I can convince them to give their permission."

"That would be great if you could do that. When do you plan on returning?"

"I have another week at the museum, and I'll leave shortly after that. I'm so glad everything's coming together for you. I hope you get the job you're looking for."

"Thank you. Keep in touch."

Although the first week back at the museum had flown by, the second week seemed to drag on forever. Still, she continued working the same hours, and she wondered how long she could keep going at that pace. When the last day of work did arrive, Sean took a little time to have a going away party for Sarah. Lunch was catered, and Sean had bought a big cake with *We'll Miss You* stenciled on top. Several people brought gifts. Some were African themed while others were things that Sarah might not be able to find in Kenya. Inez hugged her, crying. Sarah would miss her, but Inez and the temp who would take Sarah's place had struck up a quick friendship. The temp had worked out great, and Sarah knew the museum would be in good hands. She didn't feel so bad now about leaving on such short notice at such a crucial time. Everything was ahead of schedule, and they could see the light at the end of the tunnel.

Sarah took the next day getting everything packed. Wesley came over to help. She wasn't taking much with her. Wesley offered to take the items to Goodwill that she wasn't taking with her. She had put her house on the market soon after arriving back in the States, and she would have to wait on scheduling most of the utilities to stop until after she sold her house. She might have to make another trip back once the house sold, but she would worry about that when the time came. She would leave the furniture in the house. Wesley went with her to sell her car to a used car lot. He drove separately so that he could drive her home, and he even offered to take her to the airport on the day she left, which she appreciated immensely. Once she checked her bags, she kissed Wesley on the cheek, and they wished each other well. As Wesley left, Sarah saw that part of her life leave with him. She tried not to be sad; a new adventure awaited her. She wasn't leaving behind many friends, and she felt that she would see Wesley again, as a friend, of course. Soon, she was on the first flight of several that would take her to Nairobi where she would rent a car to get to the camp. Not knowing where she stood with Jack, she didn't want to ask him or Jill to pick her up. Besides, she wanted to surprise Jack, for good or bad.

Chapter 21

It was a normal day at Powell's African Camp and Safari, and Jill looked through a pile of mail as Jack stood nearby. "Here's a package from Sarah." Jack looked over briefly but soon turned back to stare at the landscape. "Sarah sent the article that Wesley published."

Jack scowled as he turned to face Jill. "That's the nail in our coffin. You might as well throw it away." Then he returned his attention back to the landscape.

"I will not! She said she was going to try to get Wesley to write a positive story."

"She may have just told you that because that's what you wanted to hear. Even if she did try to get him to write something positive, I doubt he would. He's too interested in furthering his career no matter who he hurts."

"Why do you always have to be so cynical?"

"Because of the real world. You tried to be positive when we were sent to England. You know how that turned out."

"Well, you have a point, but I don't think she would have sent this if she hadn't succeeded." Jack kept silent, and Jill sat down and began silently reading the article. After a few minutes, she finished reading and then laid it on a table. "You need to read this." She walked away leaving Jack alone.

After a few minutes, Jack mumbled to himself. "Might as well get this over with." He sat down at the table, picked up the article, and began to read.

I originally set out to tell a much different story than the one I'm about to tell. It was a story of colonialism and trophy hunting at its worst. Instead, contrary to my usual style, I'm about to tell a story of love and redemption …

Jack continued reading until he had finished. Then, he bounded out of his chair and ran to find Jill. "Jill! Jill!" He ran to a few places before finally running into the social tent with the article in his hand and finding her there. "I don't believe this. He actually painted us in a positive light."

"I told you that you needed to have faith in Sarah. She said she would try, and she definitely succeeded."

"She definitely did!" Jack relished in his excitement for several seconds before growing melancholy. "I'm afraid that my stubbornness and insecurity have cost me the woman I love. What do I do?"

"You call her, tell her what an idiot you've been, and ask her for a second chance."

At that moment, the landline phone for the camp rang, and Jack answered. "Hello. This is the Powell's African Camp and Safari. How may I help you?" Jack listened closely to the voice on the other end. "I'll be there within a couple of days." He hung up the phone, and Jill looked inquisitively at him.

"What was that about, and where are you going? I thought you were going to call Sarah."

"That was our cousin, Catherine Wells. She wants to see us. I told her I would go."

Anger spread over Jill's face, which grew red almost instantly. "I can't face that woman, and you don't have to go either!"

Before Jack could respond, Gacoki ran into the tent. "Jill, you have to come quick. We're getting more calls and emails than we can handle. They're all asking about booking a stay here."

The anger on Jill's face quickly dissipated and was replaced by a look of pure joy. "It looks like the article is already paying off." Gacoki had already left, and Jill got up and quickly ran after him. Jack pulled out his cell phone and pulled up Sarah's number. Then he turned it off and stuck it back into his pocket.

Jack left for Nairobi the next day to catch a flight to London. From there he rented a car and drove to the estate of Catherine Wells. When he arrived at the estate, it was vaguely familiar. He remembered the first time he had been there with his sister, Jill. Today was only the second time he had seen it. He didn't have fond memories of this place and his cousin, and he was hesitant to go to the door. His memory of his cousin was sketchy; if he were to see her on the street, he wouldn't recognize her. He knew she wouldn't recognize him because she hadn't seen him since he was a teenager. Yet, he came all this way. Curiosity had pushed him to come.

Might as well bite the bullet, he thought to himself, and getting out of the car he walked to the door and rang the doorbell. As big as the house was, he expected a butler or some servant to answer the door. He waited about a minute. Catherine knew he was coming today. Was she home? That would really be irritating if he came all this way to be shunned. Finally, the door slowly opened, and he was surprised to see that Catherine was the one who opened the door. The elderly woman who stood before him didn't quite fit the image in his memory, but he recognized enough of her features to know that it was her.

"Please come in, Jack!" The raspy voice of age seemed excited to see him. That was definitely different from his recollection of their first meeting all those years ago. She had to be in her eighties, probably late eighties. Her hair was white as snow, and her thin skin would have matched if not for the age spots and blue, blood veins showing on her hands and arms. She managed to move well, no obvious dexterity issues.

"Hello, Catherine." As he walked inside, he stole a quick look around. The house was large but not immaculate. It was what you would expect of an elderly person living alone. Apparently, she didn't have a large staff of servants. Surely, she didn't clean the house by herself though.

Catherine led Jack to a sitting room, which Jack remembered from his first visit when Jill and he were scared to death at first meeting their stern cousin. This time, a tray with a teapot and teacups were sitting on a table.

"I thought you would probably arrive at teatime; so, I made a pot. It should still be warm enough to be drinkable, but I can make a fresh pot if you wish."

"Oh, this will be fine."

"I'm sorry, it's not a formal tea. I gave that up years ago."

Although Jack knew he was probably violating the rules of polite conversation, he was too curious not to ask. "So, do you live here by yourself?"

"Yes. I pay someone to come and clean once a week. I gave up cleaning years ago too." She smiled a toothy smile. "One entire wing is closed off though. The entire estate is just too much to keep up. Please have a seat. Do you mind pouring the tea?" Catherine sat in a chair across from Jack.

"Not at all." Jack poured each of them a cup. "Would you like cream or lemon?"

"I just drink mine plain these days but help yourself."

Jack didn't usually drink tea, and when he did, he usually drank it plain. Today though, he thought he would go all out and add both cream and lemon. "When was this house built, if you don't mind me asking?"

"It was originally built in 1701 by the fourth Earl of Halifax. Of course, there have been renovations and modernizations since then."

Catherine took a sip of tea. By her facial expression, the tea was probably a little too tepid for her taste, but she took another sip. "Well, I don't suppose you came all of this way for a history lesson on the house or to have small talk with someone you haven't seen in over fifteen years, or has it been over twenty? I've lost count. That's what happens when you get older; time plays tricks on you. You've got a way to go before that happens to you though." She took another sip of tea. Jack imagined that whatever she wanted to say was probably difficult, maybe as difficult as it was for Jack to come here, and he felt empathy for her. She held the saucer neatly in her lap as she no doubt had done since she was a child. "Thank you for coming to England. I'm sure you're wondering why I wanted to see you."

"Receiving your call was definitely a shock. To be quite honest, I started not to come. I've only seen you once before today. That was when you sent Jill and I to a boarding school in Australia without even telling us how we were related to you? The people you sent us to in Australia were relatives of your husband, correct?"

"Yes. Graham Wells was my husband. He passed away after we had been married for twenty years. We were childless. I sent you to his brother, Dennis Wells, and his wife, Joyce." Catherine paused to take another sip of tea before continuing. "I couldn't have blamed you if you hadn't come, and I don't blame Jill for not coming. I'm sure it was quite difficult to even think about coming to see me. Since we're being honest, which I'm glad we are since that's the only way we can accomplish anything of substance, when I was informed that I was your closest relative, I didn't want to have anything to do with you or Jill."

Jack reminded himself to be calm and to approach this as an

outside observer. "Why was that? Were you just not comfortable raising teenagers?"

"That was part of it. Do the math. Even at that time I was fairly old to be raising two teenagers who didn't know me from Queen Elizabeth. But the bigger truth was that I actually hated you both."

Despite trying to be a casual outside observer, that statement rattled Jack causing him to set his teacup a little heavily on the saucer, causing a tinging noise and spilling a little tea into the saucer.

Catherine looked at Jack's reaction. "I know that's a strong feeling to have towards someone one has never met. Please hear me out," she urged. "You said you didn't know how we were related. My father was the Lord Anthony Montagu, the Earl of Halifax."

"Amelia's brother!" The revelation sent a wave of shock through Jack. He had not expected that.

"Yes. Her decision to remain in Africa and not marry the Marquess of Brackley coupled with the dubious circumstances surrounding the Marquess of Brackley's death made our family social outcasts."

"But you were born long after all that happened."

"You're right. I didn't experience any of that first-hand. I was a baby when my parents were killed. They died in the bombings of London during World War II. What is heartbreaking was that they were killed in early May of 1941, just days before the bombings ended. I was raised by my paternal grandmother, Jack and Amelia's mother, who indoctrinated me at an early age with hatred for her daughter, Amelia."

"I'm sure your mother was angry that Amelia broke off the engagement with the Marquess of Brackley and married an American with no title or riches. And as her descendants, you hated us by association?"

"That's an accurate assessment."

"So, what changed? Or has anything changed?"

"I read the article about your camp that was recently published." She paused, tears welling in her eyes, but she carried on. "I cried when I read it. I never heard that side of the story, never even thought about it to be honest. As I said, I was indoctrinated with hatred from an early age. The bad thing about hate, it is the opposite of love. Now, I know that it is an obvious statement to make. According to the Bible, love is being as concerned with another's welfare as much as your own. Hate doesn't even allow one to think about another's welfare or life circumstances. But that article sparked something within me. I remember my grandmother having some of my father's belongings stored that she could never get rid of. In fact, they were stored in the part of the estate that is closed off. I went through those belongings for the first time after reading the article and found several letters of correspondence between my father and aunt. In her reply letters, she would send back my father's letter to her. So, I have both sides of the correspondence. Plus, I found a final letter that was written by my father that he was never able to mail to Amelia. It was written just days before he was killed. I don't know why he didn't send it before he left for London or what was so urgent that required him to go to London. Unfortunately, for whatever reason, he never mailed it."

"Would you mind showing those to me?"

"I will. On a side note, I called this Wesley Baldwin who wrote the article. He asked for permission to see the letters and possibly use them in a biographical novel about Gordon Powell. I gave him my permission to write it and told him I would send him the letters, or at least copies of the letters. I told him he would need your permission as well as Jill's permission to write it, and he said he planned to ask both of you. He promised it would be a positive book, nothing scandalous and said he would even sign a document pledging that. To get to the point I wanted to make though, when you read the final letter that was never sent, you will discover that my father knew that I, being female, couldn't inherit his peerage, and he wanted Amelia's son to inherit it. My grandmother would rather the peerage become extinct than for it to pass to Amelia's son. With Anthony's death, that line of peerage did become extinct." Catherine's mouth trembled, and it was a full minute before she could continue speaking. "You could have been an earl, Jack."

Jack felt sorry for the obvious pain that Catherine was going through. "I'm happy with my life the way it is."

"I read all of the letters between them. I was surprised my grandmother kept them to be honest. I was so moved by the love my father and aunt shared. There was no blame, only love and concern. Jack, I want to apologize for the way I treated you and Jill. It's late to ask for forgiveness, but at my age, it's what I need." She looked, teary-eyed into Jack's eyes, and he could see the pleading look in her eyes. That look melted Jack's insides, and he couldn't help but forgive her.

"I forgive you, and I'm sure Jill will too."

Tears trickled down Catherine's cheek. "Thank you, Jack. You know. The British, the English especially, pride themselves in having a stiff upper lip. There's a time for that. World War II was such a time, but there's something therapeutic about showing emotion as well. You'll discover that too when you get older. Only, I hope you're wise enough to realize that before you get to be my age."

"Actually, you're teaching me that as we speak. Thank you for that."

"Now, about your camp …"

Chapter 22

Jack arrived back at Powell's African Safari and Camp tired but feeling much relieved, and he felt like a new person. The conversation he had with Catherine was not only informative but very therapeutic. He felt as though a tremendous burden had been lifted from his shoulders. The emotional baggage he carried was bigger than he believed. The conversation had been therapeutic for Catherine as well. He understood her side for the first time. Catherine's comment about being concerned about another's well-being as much as your own resonated with Jack, and he hoped he could keep that message in his heart. For one, he needed to forgive Wesley. He had thought the worst about him, but he really was an outstanding person. If it weren't for Wesley, his life wouldn't have changed for the better. Sarah could do much worse than being with Wesley. Not calling Sarah, at least in the short term, might be for the best. He would like to eventually call, as a friend, to see how she was doing, but he didn't want to intrude on the relationship she had with Wesley. A pang settled in his heart. He loved Sarah, but if she loved someone else, he would have to deal with it.

As soon as Jack got out of his jeep, Jill was there waiting for him. "We've got more business than we can handle, thanks to Wesley's article. I'll tell you more about it later, but how did things go with Catherine?"

"Surprisingly well. I know you weren't able to face her, and I understand your decision not to go, but I wish you had. I left feeling better than I have in … well, I don't know how long. She wanted forgiveness, and giving it lifted a burden from me that I was completely unaware of. I understood her motives a lot better as well, not that I'm condoning her actions. She wants your forgiveness as well. I hope that you will forgive her."

"I will. You're right. Even if I don't understand why she did what she did, I don't wish her harm. Forgiving is the right thing to do. Did she tell you why she sent us to Australia?"

"I'll get to that. But first, do you want me to tell you how we are related to her?"

"Sure. I've always wondered."

"Get this. Catherine is Anthony's daughter."

Jack waited for the shock of what he said to wear off. Jill was speechless. Her eyes and mouth were wide open. After several seconds, she blurted, "What?"

"Yep. That's right. She's Anthony's daughter."

"After all of the information we discovered about Gordon and Amelia, why did we not suspect that. I mean … she had to be related to us either on our mother's or father's side. And if we were related on our father's side, and she lived in England, then that should have at least made us wonder."

"In all fairness, we only found out about Amelia just recently. It's not like we knew all along."

"But still." Jill hesitated. I suppose I had so much anger and resentment bottled inside regarding Catherine Wells that it blinded me from even realizing that as a possibility."

Jack told Jill what Catherine had told him about her grandmother's hatred toward Amelia and about Anthony's peerage ending with his death.

"I can't imagine you being an earl," laughed Jill.

"Neither can I. I've been wondering though. Why did Dennis and Joyce Wells never tell us about how we were related to Catherine? I wish I would have thought to ask her that question."

"Well, think about it. I think they did try one time, but we shut the conversation down. We were so cross with Catherine that we didn't care. I imagine they decided to wait until we were ready to ask on our own, and that time never came. It could have also been that they were so aware of Catherine's animosity toward Amelia, and us as her descendants, that they decided against telling us. Telling a teenager that their only known relative held a grudge against them couldn't be easy."

"I want us to go back and see Catherine more often."

"Ok. We will. Being alone can't be good for her. Maybe she should sell her house and move to a retirement community. She could come here, but this is not a place for someone used to comfort and luxury."

"Well, I did have an idea I shared with her that she didn't seem opposed to." Jack paused for effect.

"Do tell. Don't keep me in suspense."

"I advised her to see an attorney and a financial consultant about turning the house into a historical site and allowing tours. The house is huge, and she had one whole section closed off. She could stay in a couple of rooms and let the rest of the house be open to public tours."

Jill raised one eyebrow and stared at Jack. "I can't believe *Mr. Don't Change Anything Ever* would even think of such an idea."

"As I keep telling you, I've never been opposed to the ideas that you and Gacoki had. I just thought it would take more than that for us to be successful. But think about it. That would allow the house to be preserved while others did the upkeep, and it would provide an income stream for her, not that she seems to need one. Plus, she wouldn't be as alone. She would at least have the company of the tour guides when they weren't busy."

"I have to hand it to you. That is rather an ingenious idea. Maybe Gacoki and I are wearing off on you!"

"If Wesley hadn't written that article, we would have gone to our graves with animosity toward her and she toward us. By the way, Wesley wants to write a biographical novel about Gordon Powell. Catherine talked with him and gave him her permission, but she said he should get ours as well. His article sparked her to look through Anthony's belongings and she found numerous letters between Anthony and Amelia. It was like a treasure trove, and we read through most of them. She sent Wesley copies, and I have copies as well that we can read. I bet Sarah will love seeing those." Jack immediately grew quiet and thought about Sarah.

"Speaking of Sarah, have you called her yet?"

Jack explained his decision not to call Sarah and the reasons behind the decision.

Jill shook her head and frowned. "I think you're making a big mistake, but I can't force you to do something you're against. I also know you're wrong about Sarah's feelings for Wesley. She told me she loved you."

"Like I said before, I blew my chance with her. She hasn't called since she left, and she certainly isn't here."

"Maybe she's waiting for you to make the first move. Don't be so proud that you lose the best thing in your life. It's great that the relationship with Catherine has been repaired, but you need someone in your life besides me."

Chapter 23

Sarah was driving on the familiar dirt road to the camp. The sign that said *Private Road* had been cleared of vegetation and was clearly visible this time. The gate was closed, but the lock had been left open. She was glad the lock was open. She wanted to surprise Jack in person, not call him and ask to be let in. Thoughts of reuniting with Jack flooded her mind. Hopefully, he was no longer mad at her, but did he still love her or at least have strong feelings for her? Those thoughts were interrupted by a sudden vibration coming from the rental car. The vibration startled her, and then she realized what had caused it … a flat tire. "Not again! How is this even possible? What dumb fortune."

Sarah gradually brought the car to a stop and got out to verify her suspicion. The tires were good on her side. When she walked around to the passenger side, she saw the flat tire. A frustrating and heavy sigh escaped her mouth. She blew the hair out of her eyes. Thinking about the last time this had happened, she fearfully looked around to see if a lion or any other carnivorous animal were in sight. Seeing none, she pulled out her phone. She would have to call Jack after all. So much for the surprise. Maybe she could call Jill or Gacoki instead and still be able to surprise Jack. She tried calling Jill, but the phone was silent. She looked at her phone and noticed that she didn't have a signal. "No signal. That's just great." She wondered what to do. She could either try walking up the road until she was able to get a signal or get in her car and wait hopefully for someone to come along. Neither option seemed ideal. Walking alone when wild animals were potentially present wasn't smart, but sitting in her car possibly overnight until someone might pass by the next day was no better. She tried to remember which days the safari jeep traveled this road, but she was tired and frustrated, which clouded her thinking. Suddenly, the solution came to mind … change the tire. She had never changed a tire before. She promised herself the last time this happened that she would learn. But she had been so busy when she returned to Colorado with working at the museum and getting ready to come back that the promise had escaped her mind. She would have to at least try. Fear entered her mind again. What if a lion came up behind her while she was changing the tire? She involuntarily shuttered at the thought.

While Sarah was studying the tire and thinking about the steps she should take to change the tire, a jeep pulled up behind her car and stopped. Sarah was lost in thought, and her mind didn't register the sound of the jeep.

Jack stepped out of the jeep, left the door open so as to not make any additional noise, and stealthily approached the car, coming up behind Sarah.

"This is a private road. What are you doing here?" Sarah jerked at the sound of the voice and turned around, the blood draining from her face leaving her face ashen. "Didn't you see the gate and the sign?" Jack continued, wearing a broad grin.

"The color returning to her face, Sarah stood, smoothed over her clothes with her hands, and in the most serious expression and tone she could muster, replied, "I didn't see a sign."

"You didn't see the sign that said Jack is a big dummy?"

"Oh, I knew that without having to see a sign." She grinned, matching the grin on Jack's face.

"And you came anyway?"

"Yes. I came back because I love this stubborn man. You may know him. His name is Jack Powell."

"Oh, him. I know him well, and yes, he is very stubborn, but he loves you very much too."

Both ran the short distance to each other and held each other tightly.

"I want to kiss you, but I don't want to let go," cooed Sarah.

"Who says you have to let go to kiss me?"

Both moved their heads to stare into the other's eyes, still clinging tightly to each other. Without further hesitation, they kissed. All of Sarah's fears vanished, and she felt safe and at peace, perhaps truly for the first time in her life.

"I'll never doubt you again," swore Jack, breaking off the kiss but still holding Sarah tightly.

"I'm going to hold you to that."

"I like the holding part, almost as much as the kissing part. Are you here for good? What about your job at the museum?"

"I quit my job at the museum. I wasn't doing what I really wanted to do, and my heart is here. Has anything happened since I've been gone?"

"Oh, has it. Because of the article, so many people have called that we can't book them all. Then I got a call from my cousin, Catherine Wells, who, as it turns out, is Anthony's daughter."

Surprise showed on Sarah's face. "The woman who sent you and Jill to a boarding school in Australia is Anthony's daughter?"

"Remarkable, isn't it? She asked for our forgiveness and gave us a hefty sum of money. To make up for Amelia being ostracized by their parents, Anthony had planned to give Amelia more money before he was killed. We can pay off the loan, add more tents, and incorporate Jill's and Gacoki's ideas.

"Did Jill find out about the property along the coast?"

"Yes. It turns out that it was included as part of the camp, but the specifics were lost along the way. We have an attorney who is clearing everything up legally. Our camp's survival is now possible thanks to Gordon and Amelia, and you."

"Is our story going to be as happy as Gordon's and Amelia's story?"

"Definitely! Hop in the jeep, and I'll ask someone to change your tire, again."

"I have to warn you. I don't have a reservation."

"Don't worry. I saved the pup tent!"

Sarah playfully elbowed Jack. "Before we get into the jeep, I think we have some unfinished business."

"Yes ma'am." Engulfing Sarah in his arms, his lips met hers and their bodies melted together as one.

Epilogue: One Year Later

The two weeks after Sarah had returned from England had gone by like a whirlwind. The first week she got back, Wesley came to spend a ten-day vacation at Powell's African Camp and Safari, and he brought his new girlfriend, a fellow reporter who worked at CNN. Wesley had gotten the job within a month of the article being published. He was now being promoted at CNN and had taken a vacation prior to the start of the new job. Sarah wondered how he had found the time to find a girlfriend.

Wesley had performed double duty working at CNN and writing a biographical novel of Gordon Powell and Kagiso, which had been released only a month ago. The book was already on the New York Times best seller list. Gacoki's grandfather had described in detail Gordon's hunting of the man-eaters, and two letters between Amelia and Anthony talked a lot about Gordon's childhood; Gordon had told Anthony and Kagiso about his childhood when they were in the field hospital. The focus of the book switched from focusing primarily on Gordon Powell to focusing on Kagiso as well. The switch on focus came when Wesley discovered some surprising information. Wesley spoke with an expert on aristocratic families, who specialized primarily in dukedoms. The expert showed Wesley a newspaper article that had been published in 1946, over twenty years after Thomas' death. The article reported on the suicide of a man and the suicide note he left behind. In the note, the man described his mental turmoil for over twenty years. He had been hunting in the African savanna in Kenya. He was an inexperienced hunter who didn't hire the services of a guide. When he heard a big rustling noise within some vegetation, he shot without thinking. He heard, what he thought was an animal collapse he went to investigate and found the body of a man bleeding profusely from his throat. Scared, he turned and fled, only to return a few minutes later. By then, a man he assumed to be Kenyan was kneeling beside of the body. He left the scene, switched to a different rifle, went to the police, and reported the shooting accident, suggesting that the Kenyan had fired the shot. With the state of police forensics not being what it was in modern times, the police quickly closed the case, ruling it a hunting accident. The man who killed Thomas indicated in his suicide note that he had carried that guilt with him ever since the shooting. What finally drove him over the edge was the death of his son, who was his only child, on June the sixth, 1944 on a beach in Normandy during Operation Overlord, or D-Day. He suffered for almost two years until he could no longer bear it, at which point he shot himself. Since so much time had passed, the article did not receive much attention. With this new information, and the fact that Kagiso wouldn't be implicated in Thomas Mowbray's death, Wesley decided to write the book about Gordon and Kagiso. He wrote about their different upbringings, their experiences in World War I, their friendship, and their experiences in Kenya after the war. Wesley couldn't help but include a narrative on colonialism and its impact, but he did so in a respectful way. Ultimately, the book was about the friendship of two people from different cultures, their sufferings, and their lives after they lost touch with each other. It was a heartfelt book.

Inez Martinez had informed Sarah that the museum was capitalizing on the book to highlight the Gordon Powell exhibit it housed. Powell's African Camp and Safari had gained even more popularity due to the book's release and was booked far in advance. Jack quickly added a new tent just to accommodate Wesley's request to visit.

Wesley and his girlfriend, Nima Kurtzman, seemed a good pair. Wesley had confided to Sarah that he planned to ask Nima to marry him soon. On this trip, Wesley and Nima took advantage of every excursion and activity the camp had to offer, far different than Wesley's first trip to the camp. He seemed a completely different person and was enjoying life as Sarah had never seen from him previously. Wesley was a hit with the fellow guests, and he shared stories from his book, which included several from the letters found by Catherine Wells between Anthony and Amelia. The day Wesley and Nima left, he booked another stay in six months. Even though the camp was booked, Jack made the reservation, telling Wesley that he was welcome any time. Sarah was surprised at how well Jack and Wesley got along with each other. One would think they were best friends.

Sarah had spent three months in England helping with the opening of Catherine Wells estate as a tourist attraction. Catherine moved to a smaller cottage on the grounds and opened the entire main house for tours. Unshackled from her former resentment, Sarah found Catherine to be a lovely and interesting person. Catherine often showed up for the tours and gave personal stories to those visiting. Even though Catherine was in her eighties, she had grown more active as the months progressed. Sarah thought she seemed truly happy.

During Sarah's three months in England, she had missed Jack terribly, only getting a brief respite when Jack and Jill had made a visit to stay for a week. Catherine had been extremely excited about their visit. Everyone seemed truly happy and renewed over their newly reestablished family. Jill had visited Catherine several months before, and the two quickly patched up their differences. Catherine had asked for Jill's forgiveness at that time, and Jill forgave her. During Jack's and Jill's visit, Catherine had mentioned to a tour group that Jack could have been the Earl of Halifax had the title not become extinct upon Anthony's death. The remainder of the week, Jack was often embarrassed when several people referred to him as Lord Powell. Even Catherine gibed Jack, referring to him on several occasions as Lord Powell, Earl of Halifax. When Sarah left, the estate was extravagant looking, and the tours were wildly popular and successful.

The staff lodge at the camp had been torn down and rebuilt. It included several guest rooms for people who didn't want to stay in the elaborate tents, living quarters for the camp's co-owners, an office, a small one room museum dedicated to Gordon and Amelia Powell where the reframed picture of Gordon and Amelia hung along with Jack's military awards. The small museum also included pictures of famous guests from the past. Amelia had hung the picture of her grandfather at the camp as well.

Sarah looked at the time and hurried to the meeting area where Jack was welcoming a new group of guests arriving today. As she headed to the meeting area, she thought back to her life in Colorado over a year ago. Who would have thought her life would have changed so much during this time? Not only had her life changed but the life of Wesley and those she had not even met at the time, people such as Jack, Jill, Gacoki, and Catherine. Nearing the meeting area, she could hear Jack giving his usual welcoming remarks.

"During your stay here, you can participate in lots of activities. We truly have something for everyone: our traditional jeep safari tour, a hot air balloon ride over the savanna, a Maasai warrior-led hike to a waterfall, a visit to a nearby Maasai village where you will see the culture of the Maasai, a conversancy and rehabilitation area to reintroduce orphaned and hurt animals back into the wild, a traditional canvas bush bath on your veranda, great food and private dining if you wish, a dining and social tent fashioned in the style of the 1920s, coffee tasting, stargazing, and professional photography to allow you to always remember your experiences here. Also, a portion of your registration fees goes to the Maasai village, and our staff includes several people from the Maasai village who have chosen to work here. If you have any questions, we're here to help." Jack paused and turned to point to Jill and Gacoki. "This is my sister, Jill, and her husband, Gacoki." Jack paused again and turned to point to Sarah. The butterflies in her stomach fluttered to see the look on Jack's face as he smiled at her. "And this is my wife, Sarah, who has finished a book on the culture of the Maasai."

Sarah wondered how she had had time to do all she had done in the past year.

A young man in the group who appeared to be in his early twenties raised his hand, and Jack acknowledged him. "We're on our honeymoon," declared the young man who turned to his wife and smiled, "and we also booked a few nights at a hut on the beach."

Gacoki stepped forward to address the man. "We have that noted on your reservation, and we'll provide the transportation to and from the beach hut." Gacoki turned to face the group. "Now, our staff will show you to your accommodations. Once you get settled, dinner will be served in the dining tent in one hour. If you get settled earlier, please feel free to stop by the social tent and ask our bartender for a drink. We have several unique cocktails, along with wine and beer, that will suit a variety of tastes."

Several staff members led the guests to their tents.

Sarah walked over to Jack, and he put his arm around her. "You've been back for two weeks, and we've barely had any time together," stated Jack.

"We'll have to remedy that. You know. I was thinking earlier today about our wedding."

"I didn't forget our anniversary, did I?" teased Jack.

"No, and you'd better not! Our first anniversary is coming up in a little over a month."

"And you were gone three months out of our first year."

"I'll make sure that doesn't happen again."

"I would like that, but you know I want you to be happy, and doing field work in cultural anthropology makes you happy. If you need to go to Australia or somewhere to do work, I'll support you."

"You could go with me, you know."

"Now that the camp is in good shape and we have plenty of staff, I might take you up on that. So, what were you saying about our wedding?"

"Oh, I was just thinking how beautiful the ceremony was that we had at the waterfall. Hey! That gives me an idea. Maybe we should add weddings as an option!"

"That's a good idea, but Jill and Gacoki have already mentioned that."

"It figures!" Sarah replied, rolling her eyes. "I don't think they will ever run out of new ideas for the camp!"

"Getting back to our upcoming anniversary, what do you want to do?"

Sarah looked toward the setting sun on the horizon as she thought. The sky cast a fiery glow to the grassland of the savanna, and the gentle breeze made the grass appear to shimmer. I wouldn't mind going back to the beach hut."

"We can do that, especially since we added several new huts, with enough distance between them to ensure privacy."

"As long as they aren't all booked."

Jack winked. "They won't be."

"Gordon and Amelia would be proud if they could see the camp now. It is the vision of what they wanted it to be."

"And I can never thank you enough for allowing me to see the real Gordon Powell. It completely changed my perspective of him, and I'm proud that he and Amelia were my great grandparents."

"Well, I'm going to go and change before dinner."

"Why are you telling me that?"

Sarah smiled slyly, "I thought you might want to watch as I walk away."

"Any time, Ms. Powell!"

Jack leaned in and kissed Sarah. She turned and began walking away with her arm held slightly behind her. Jack grabbed her hand and followed as she made her way back to their room.

About the Author

Dewey Dellinger is an educator and administrator. He was born, raised, and lives in North Carolina and has degrees from North Carolina State University, the University of North Carolina at Charlotte, and East Carolina University. His highest degree is a Ph.D. from North Carolina State University. His novel genres include fantasy, action-adventure, romance and romantic comedy, and drama.

Books by Dewey

Once Upon a Knight's Time Series
Once Upon a Knight's Time
Once Upon a Knight's Time: Seeker of the Sword

Romance
Love's Trail in Kenya

Action Heroine
Captain Tomorrow

www.ingramcontent.com/pod-product-compliance
Lightning Source LLC
Chambersburg PA
CBHW022034240626
47154CB00007B/2407